Grown-ups Can't Be Friends With Dragons

Antony Wootten

Eskdale Publishing
www.antonywootten.co.uk
eskdalebooks@gmail.com

Eskdale Publishing, UK

First published in Great Britain in 2012 by Eskdale Publishing,
North Yorkshire

www.antonywootten.co.uk

A Catalogue record for this book is available from the British
Library.

ISBN: 978-0-9537123-3-5

**Printed and bound in the UK by York Publishing Services
www.yps-publishing.co.uk**

For my parents, who gave me

a truly magical childhood.

The Chrysalis

"What is it?" Brian asked.

"It's a baby butterfly, stupid."

"It don't look much like a butterfly to me," Brian said, peering at the little black thing. It looked a bit like a slug but was hard and shiny. It was in a flat glass dish on the 'interest table' just outside the classroom door. It was almost the end of school, and a few of the children had stopped to look at the thing when they were collecting their bags and lunch boxes. Brian pushed it round the dish with his finger.

"Leave it alone now," Terry said. "Stop touching it, Brian." He grabbed Brian's arm. "Leave off, it's mine, I found it."

"I was only looking," Brian objected crossly.

"You were touching it," Terry said. "You're not allowed to touch it."

Brian scowled and felt anger burning inside him. "It's not a butterfly," he snapped. "You're just lying. Where's its wings? It doesn't even move."

"So? Didn't you listen? Miss said it's asleep inside a chrysalis. It's changing."

"Miss is stupid then," Brian blurted. The other

children gasped.

"I'm telling Miss you called her stupid," Terry said. "Stinky Brian. You stink." Some of the other children, who had gathered nearby to watch the showdown, laughed.

"No I don't."

"Yes you do." Terry was talking in a whisper now in case any of the teachers were nearby. "I'm gonna tell Miss what you called her and she's gonna throw you out and we won't have to put up with your stink anymore!"

Brian couldn't stop himself doing what he did next. He hardly even knew he was doing it. It was as if the anger inside him had taken control of his arm, and he thumped his fist down on the chrysalis as hard as he could. It felt weird: solid, and a bit soft. It crunched. The chrysalis stuck to his hand at first, then it fell back into the dish with a clicky noise. It had split open. It looked like a rose bud which had been trodden on. Thin bits like leaves poked out of the splits in its sides. Terry shouted. Roger, who was standing nearby, began to cry, as usual, even though it was nothing to do with him.

Brian felt his face burning, and his eyes began to sting. He hated Terry. He hated school.

He ran.

He dodged past Miss as she emerged from the classroom. He slammed through the doors and charged across the playground. It was nearly the end of school and parents were already gathering at the gate. It was a warm September day.

Emily was there waiting for him. She had a cigarette in her hand. She had her school jumper tied around her waist and her school tie tied around her arm. She always sneaked out of school early to come and collect Brian, but he wished she wouldn't. He ran right past her, ignoring her shouts. She even tried to chase him, but the heel of one of her shoes broke and she swore loudly.

Brian didn't want to go home. So he kept on running, down the hill, towards the harbour.

Brian's Secret

Brian ran down the steep cliff road towards the harbour. He could smell the sea and hear the gulls crying overhead. But he hated them, and he hated everything. It was a long way and his legs started to hurt, but he hated them too and the pain felt good. He found himself going faster than he ever could on flat ground and started to feel out of control. His feet slapped the tarmac noisily and painfully and he felt that any minute now his legs would give way. But he didn't care. He just kept running.

Eventually, the road levelled out and came to an end at the car park in front of a row of stone cottages. There were a couple of boats moored against the harbour wall, bobbing gently on the waves, and as usual, all he could smell was fish.

Exhausted, he had to stop running now, and he made his way across the car park, kicking the stones as he went. It was always cooler down here in the harbour than up on top of the cliffs where the school and his house were. The car park ended where a long rocky rise stretched out from the bottom of the cliff like a wall, across the end of the car park, and into the sea. Brian was a good climber.

He clambered onto the sharp rocks, jumping the rock-pools and the dangerous gaps, over the rise and down the other side to the little shale beach there. Looking up, Brian could see the grass on the cliffs above, blowing in the wind. It made him feel very small, and very alone. But he liked it here. He had a vague memory of being here with his mum, a long time ago. He walked around on the beach and then sat down and dug a hole. He listened to the water hitting the rocks, and tried to remember what his mum looked like. There were a couple of photos of her around the house, but they were just pictures. When he actually tried to remember her, when he tried to picture her here on the beach with him that day, he couldn't see her, and he couldn't hear her voice either.

There was a cave at the other side of the beach. It was dark and cold and lonely. And it was Brian's cave. In fact, this was Brian's beach. No-one else even knew about this place, as far as he could tell. Only him, and this was where he came when he hated the world and everyone in it, including himself. He didn't always go straight into the cave. Sometimes he'd sit on the wet shale, digging, or throwing stones into the sea, or just listening to the waves and letting his own breathing fall into their rhythm, until he wasn't angry any more, just empty. Sometimes though, the beach wasn't quite far enough away from the rest of the world. That's when he wanted to be in the cave.

He left his hole and walked over to it. The cliffs towered over him and he felt himself disappear into the cave's cold darkness. The bumpy, rock floor rose out of the shale and sloped up towards the back where it was almost too dark to see, but Brian wasn't scared. He wiped his nose on his sleeve, making more 'snail trails' for Emily to moan about.

He went further in, climbing up towards the back of the cave.

Somewhere, the wind whistled through cracks and nooks. It almost sounded like someone whispering his name, welcoming him in.

He found the smooth dent in the rock where he always sat. Further back, the cave got really dark and he couldn't see where it ended. He'd sometimes wondered what was back there. One day, he would have to bring a torch down and find out.

He felt about in the dark space beside him, and found the old box of crayons he kept hidden there. Even this far into the cave, there was still enough light to see by, once his eyes adjusted, and he took a few moments to run his fingers over the drawings he'd already done on the rocky wall. They weren't very good, in fact he couldn't even tell what some of them were anymore, partly because the crayon had faded and worn away, and partly because he'd done some of them when he was younger, when he was in the lower juniors at school. Drawings he'd thought were really good back then just looked like scribbles now to his more grown up eyes.

Most of them were drawings of himself with his mum, and that's what he decided to draw today. He knew from the photos that her hair was long and wavy and she sometimes wore a yellow jumper, so that's how he drew her.

Then, he decided to add his dad too. He was much bigger than his mum. Tall and strong. He made them both have smiles. When he thought about his mum, he imagined her smiling, but it didn't look quite right seeing a smile on his dad's face. He liked it though. Lastly, he even drew Emily.

He looked at the finished drawing, and nodded.

Then he heard that noise again. The one that almost sounded like his name. It was clearer this time. It didn't quite sound like a voice, but it didn't quite sound like the wind or the sea either. It was like soft, gentle music with some deep, louder instrument over the top, and it seemed to be coming from the back of the cave.

He stared into the darkness for some time, not moving, not thinking, just waiting. He was beginning to feel cold now and something dripped on his hair. But the voice was gone, and Brian suddenly realised how hungry he was.

*

Brian stepped over the big pair of motorcycle boots and the scratched, white helmet. At least that means Mark's here, he thought as he quietly pushed the back door closed. In the kitchen, Emily had been pulling socks and pants from the washing machine and hanging them on the airer. She stopped and put her hands on her hips, and glared at him. "Where the hell have you been, Brian, you stupid little—" Brian felt his face going red. Emily always got like this when Brian had run away. He could hear the TV in the front room. Mark was probably there with his feet on the coffee table, and Brian wanted to go through and see him. Mark was never angry with him, even when he'd run away from Emily.

"I was just about to call the police!" Emily was almost yelling now and Brian wished she'd just shut up. "Your teacher wanted me to call the police," she added. "She must think I'm completely useless. She'll probably report us to Social Services or something. Dad'll kill you when he gets in. You'll be grounded for a month," she snapped, and Brian felt as if he was going to explode. At least Dad was working nights, which meant he wouldn't be back until the morning. Brian looked up at Emily and hoped she wouldn't notice the tears which were stinging his eyes. But then Emily couldn't talk anymore because she was starting to cry. She bent down and hugged him, and the burning anger in his stomach flowed away. He knew he should apologise now, and he wanted to, but somehow, he couldn't. He couldn't even return her hug. She stank of cigarettes. "Do you know the worry you've caused?" She stood up again, her chin crumpling, and Brian looked at her, guiltily. There were dark bits on her cheeks where her makeup had run. Brian knew it was his fault; Emily hadn't done anything to deserve this. He felt sick again, but in a different way this time; it wasn't anger anymore, just a horrible feeling, and he didn't know what to say.

"Well, where have you been?" she asked, calmer now. Brian didn't want to tell her. She asked again, and he shrugged, but he didn't mean it rudely. "Don't shrug at me! Where've you been?"

"I dunno," he said quietly. The cave was his secret.

"Oh, I give up," Emily sighed. "I really do. I give up. Don't blame me if you get taken into care, Bri," she said, but then she started crying again. She pressed her face into the rag in her hand, realised it was her dad's pants, and slammed them down crossly on the work top. Brian suddenly felt he was going to laugh, but he wasn't ready to be friendly yet. So he turned away and went into the front room.

Mark, Emily's boyfriend, was slumped in the big

chair, his feet on the coffee table as usual. He had long hair that was tied back in a ponytail, and a couple of big shiny earrings in one ear. Without turning his eyes from the TV, he said, "Guess you're in trouble then, mate." Mark was nearly always at Brian's house. Sometimes he even slept there, but Brian wasn't allowed to tell his dad that. "Went looking all over for you, you know."

"On your motorbike?" Brian asked, wondering if he'd missed the chance of a ride. Emily wouldn't ever let Mark take him for a ride on his motorbike, but it would be different if Mark found him somewhere on his own and had to bring him back.

"Yes, mate. Down the harbour, then up on the estates. Where were you this time?"

Brian walked over to him.

"What you watching?" he asked as the sound of gun fire exploded from the TV. Mark liked scary films, and Brian didn't want to look.

"Em was worried sick, Bri. She nearly called the Old Bill." Brian wondered what would have happened if she did. Would he get put in prison? Or maybe he'd get taken to live with a different family like Emily often said. He didn't really want to leave Emily, Mark and his dad, but he daydreamed sometimes about living in a big house with a different family. Perhaps he could even have a brother or sister his own age. A dog. A mum!

"I knew you'd come back when you were ready though, Bri," Mark said, his eyes still fixed on the burbling TV behind Brian.

"What you watching?" Brian asked again. He sat on the sofa and watched two men charging headlong down an alleyway between dark buildings.

"Oh, a movie, it's not really for children though," he said. For a moment, it seemed as though Mark was more interested in his film than in Brian, but just as Brian was trying to think of something to say, Mark reached over and rubbed his strong hand all over Brian's head. Brian laughed and curled away, batting Mark's hand, and Mark said, "Oh, it's like that is it? Come on then, squirt!" and got up from his chair. He leaned over and pretended to try and slap Brian's cheek. Brian parried the attack, but wasn't ready for Mark's other hand which caught him a playful blow across the head. Brian laughed and complained at the same time, and Mark suddenly whirled round and got Brian into a headlock, shoving his face into the sofa cushions. Brian wriggled, but Mark was strong, and all Brian could do was to free his face from the cushion and look instead at the pictures on Mark's leather jacket. He loved the smell of it, and the way it felt cold against his hot face. Mark manoeuvred himself so that he was sitting on the sofa and could carry on watching the film whilst keeping Brian playfully pinned down.

"Ooh, good bit coming up, Bri," he taunted, knowing Brian couldn't see the screen. "Ooh, it's amazing, you've never seen anything like it!" Brian couldn't help laughing. Mark's grip wasn't tight, but he was happy to lie there pretending he couldn't move.

"Mark!" Emily snapped as she came into the front room. "What do you think you're doing? He can't watch this."

"I don't think he can see it, Em," Mark said.

"No, but... it's not the point," she objected. "Turn it off."

From his uncomfortable position, Brian made a feeble attempt to free himself, but succeeded only in pressing his face deeper into a fold of Mark's jacket where it was dark and cold, just like in his cave. He felt Emily drop herself onto the sofa beside him.

"Alright," Mark said, and Brian could tell he had leaned over and kissed her. Then the TV's frightening sounds stopped suddenly and became the evening news instead. "You phoned his teacher to say he's back?"

Emily sighed. "I'll do it in a bit." Brian imagined her arms folded and her face scowling. "He hates me, Mark," she said. There was a silence, and Brian knew he should tell her that wasn't true, but he didn't. "So where did you go then?" she asked Brian, but Brian didn't reply. "See?" Emily said to Mark, who seemed just as engrossed in the news as he had been in his film. "Mark!"

"Yes, love?" Mark said softly. But Emily just let out a moan and stomped back out to the kitchen.

Eventually, Mark released Brian from his headlock, and Brian slumped beside him, gazing at the pictures on his leather jacket. It was covered in them. Mark painted the pictures himself. Brian loved the wizard on the back with magic lights coming out of his fingers, but he couldn't see that at the moment. On one shoulder was a dragon, delicately painted in white, the black leather showing through for the shadows. The eyes were dark, but two glinting points of light made them look real.

Mark was always adding to the pictures, changing them or removing them and painting new ones. There'd been a dolphin there for a while. Mark said he'd done it for Emily, because she loves dolphins. The picture reminded Brian of a sad story Emily had told him once about a dolphin becoming lost. It was true, and had happened years ago, before Brian was born. It had swum into the harbour and couldn't find its way back to its family and friends. Fishermen, and some scientists, had tried to help it, but the poor thing didn't understand. In the end, it had died. On days like today, when he was in trouble and the whole world seemed angry with him, he often found himself thinking about the poor, lonely dolphin, all lost.

Dragon

Despite Emily's prediction, Dad didn't kill him; he just looked very disappointed and sad. He did ground him though.

The next day, Miss Neale spoke gently to Brian about what had happened, and he told her he was sorry. She made him look at her and she held his hands as she spoke to him. He could smell her perfume; it reminded him of something from so long ago he couldn't quite tell what it was, but somehow it made him feel warm and cosy even though he was being told off.

After school, it was his dad who picked him up. Brian caught that familiar whiff which told him he had been to the pub. He was a tall man, and though he put his hand affectionately on Brian's shoulder, he didn't say much to him, and Brian felt it was best to keep quiet too.

After tea, Dad left for work while Emily was still washing up, and a short while later, Brian heard Mark's motorbike pulling up outside. After a while, Emily and Mark went upstairs. Brian could hear them laughing in Emily's room, but he knew they wanted to be on their own. He was bored of the TV, so he put his dad's old torch in his coat pocket and sneaked out of the back door. He didn't care about being grounded. Maybe Mark would come looking for him on his motorbike later.

The harbour was quiet, and it was just starting to get dark. There were two fishing boats tied to the big stone sea-wall that curved round the harbour. The wall had two different levels you could walk on, and it was wide enough for small vans to park on it while the fishermen loaded or unloaded their boats. There were a few small, white houses where the wall began. And a pub. Brian's dad liked to go in there a lot, but it made Brian feel uneasy. He wasn't sure why.

He was eager to get to his cave. In his cave, no-one could upset him. No-one even knew it existed. He went across the empty car park and climbed over the rocks to the little shale beach. It was already quite dark inside the cave now. He got the torch out, pleased with himself for thinking to bring it this time, and climbed up to the high place at the back. Even though the rock was damp and cold, he still felt strangely snug, comforted by the darkness and the sound of the waves and a distant memory of perfect happiness. He drew himself playing football with Gary, one of the popular boys in his class.

The wind was making its funny noises just like before. It sounded as if it was singing in the dark place behind him. He listened.

And then it said his name. Just like before, the voice was friendly and welcoming and musical, and he listened for it to call him again.

"Brian... Brian," the wind's voice sang gently.

"Hello?" He said, excited.

"Brian..."

He shone his torch around. He could not see very much. He shook the torch but the batteries must have been running out.

"Hello?" he said, a bit louder than before. "Where are you?"

"Brian," the strange, calm voice said, and it gave him a warm feeling of comfort. He turned and shone the torch behind where he was sitting. He could see nothing but rock, but that was where the voice was coming from. The cave floor sloped upwards in big lumps, until it met the jagged roof.

He climbed until he found himself in a space that he hadn't noticed before, high up and right at the back where the cave was utterly dark. The rock glistened as he waved the thin torch beam over it. The voice called him on, and he noticed a patch in the rock which stayed black even when he shone the torch right at it. He waved his hand in it and found it was a gap, big enough for him to get into. Assuming it must lead somewhere, he swung himself round so his feet were in the gap, and lowered himself until he could feel solid rock under his foot. He slid himself down onto a small ledge, and clambered further down over bumpy rock, until he was in what seemed to be a tunnel.

He was on a smooth, flat floor. Down here, the walls of the tunnel were different from the cave walls. The tunnel's walls, and the floor, were straight and flat, like inside a building. Not at all like the wobbly, sloping, curving walls of the cave. But they had amazing patterns on them. He realised this was strange, but he didn't feel scared. He felt excited, and *welcome*, as if this was somewhere he was *supposed* to be. Swirls and spirals and strange shapes made up the patterns, and he stood there and looked closely at them for ages.

Then the voice called him again. He'd almost forgotten about it, but, excited again, he hurried on towards it. The tunnel started to slope downwards now. He kept stopping to look at the patterns. He touched them, they were raised and bumpy like the paint on Mark's jacket.

There were some big, knobbly, pointed mounds on the floor with water dripping on them from above. They didn't look like part of the tunnel. The tunnel was flat and square, as if someone had built it, but these were more like something that had grown, like upside down icicles. Some of them were nearly as tall as him, and wide as the tree in the playground. Brian remembered Miss Neale telling them that lumps like that often grew inside caves, sometimes from the floor and sometimes from the ceiling. The torch beam flickered a bit. He hoped it wasn't going to stop working.

Then he felt the tunnel around him change. He couldn't see the walls anymore, and the air felt cooler. Even with the torch he could hardly see anything except the floor, but somehow he could tell he had come into a very big, wide space, like inside a church perhaps. This place smelt different. Cleaner, not so much like the sea. And the voice kept calling him.

He could hear echoes of his footsteps now. They sounded as though they were coming from a long way off. The smooth floor sloped sideways here; it was like walking on the side of a hill and he slipped over once or twice. In the torch beam, he could just about make out water at the bottom of the slope. Slowly, straining his eyes, he crossed the cavern. And he came to the wall at the far side. He could see more swirly patterns in the torch light. He stayed close to the wall, and walked up the slope, towards the voice.

There was a small, black space part way up the wall, like a window or an entrance to something. More of the knobbly things—stalagmites, he remembered now—blocked the entrance a bit, and the voice was coming from inside it. He climbed up and squeezed through the gaps into the hole. It was like a small cave, quite dry, and cold.

"Hello!" The voice was friendly, and it was very close. He shone the torch around, and this time the beam glowed back at him from two curved, glassy objects, round, and roughly the size of large pebbles. They were right in front of him, and he realised they were eyes. He could hardly see the creature they belonged to at all; just the wide, dark, unblinking eyes, and he wasn't scared. He was just... interested, and excited.

"Hello?" he said, sitting down and looking at the eyes. As he shone the torch closer and around them he could see what looked like soft, white skin, but the torch beam was too weak to cut through the thick blackness of this place. Whatever this creature was though, it didn't seem to be very big, and Brian knew straight away that it was not going to hurt him. He also realised now that this was all very strange.

"Woah!" he said, peering closer. "What are you?"

"I am..." the voice said, but it stopped, as if it didn't know the answer to the question. "Something hurts," it said then. "It's too..."

"Are you injured? Do you need help?" Brian was suddenly worried. Had this creature called him here to help it? He angled the torch's feeble glow at the creature and tried to see what was wrong. He now saw there were strange tubes and pipes all around it, he could vaguely make out that the creature was loosely wrapped in them.

"...Too bright," the creature said, a note of pain in its voice, and Brian realised it was referring to the torch.

"Oh, sorry," he said, and switched it off. Now he was sitting there in that tiny, dark alcove at the back of a huge underground cavern, in total darkness. In fact, it wasn't just dark, it was a thick, cold blackness that it almost made his eyes hurt, so he shut them, and that seemed to soothe them.

"Thank you," the creature said.

"It's okay, I didn't mean to hurt your eyes."

"I know."

Brian didn't know what to say then. Somehow, just being here felt right, and even though the rock he was sitting on was cold, this tiny little hole in the cavern wall felt cosy.

"So, what *are* you?" Brian asked again. "Why are you here?"

"I'm..." said the creature. "I'm..." Brian waited, like Miss Neale did for him when he was trying to read a difficult word in his reading book. "I'm... I don't know. I don't... know."

"You don't know who you are?" Brian asked, surprised, and then thought that might have been rude, so said, "It doesn't matter. Maybe I can help you." He thought for a moment, and then said, "Maybe you're a cat. Or a dog." It made sense to him that someone's pet might have wandered in here and got itself stuck. But, at the same time, he could see this was clearly no ordinary animal and he was embarrassed for having made such a stupid suggestion. The creature said nothing. Perhaps it was thinking about it. "Do you need me to get you out?" Brian said.

"No," the creature replied. "This is where I live. This is where I have always lived."

Brian suddenly knew what it was, though it didn't quite look like pictures he'd seen. Especially the one on Mark's jacket. "You're a sort of dragon aren't you?" he said. "Dragons live in caves by the sea! Like in that song we sing at school."

"Maybe that's what I am," the creature said.

"I think you are a dragon," he said. "Are you sure you don't need me to help you get out? Are you stuck?"

The creature seemed to laugh.

"Why are you laughing?" Brian said.

"You are asking me if I need help. But *you* called to *me* for help."

Now Brian was really confused. "I didn't call you. I don't need help with anything. Except my spelling and reading sometimes, but Miss Neale helps me with that. *You* called *me*. That's why I came."

The creature didn't say anything for a while. Brian thought perhaps he was thinking about something. Then the creature said, "I have been here so long I have forgotten myself."

"Forgotten yourself?"

"It was as if I had drifted away. I have had no thoughts for a very long time. I have known only darkness and emptiness."

"Do you mean you've been asleep?"

"Yes, sort of. For a very long time." He said lots of other strange things too, and Brian didn't really understand what he meant. He just liked listening to him. His voice was like music, like the violins they listened to on the stereo in assembly. After a while, Brian realised the dragon wasn't talking anymore. His words seemed to have turned into a tune.

"What are you singing?" Brian asked.

"A song. I can remember songs. Would you like to hear more?"

"Yes please," he said.

Brian always liked singing at school, but the dragon's singing was different. It didn't really have words, just a strange, winding, twisting tune. It seemed as though the creature had lots of voices, like a choir, and each voice sang a slightly different tune. Brian was transfixed. It was the most beautiful music he'd ever heard, and it reminded him of something. It reminded him of the patterns on the tunnel walls he'd seen earlier. The lines and shapes seemed to wind around each other in the same way as the dragon's many voices did. Then, something else came into his head. It was like a cross between sound and colour and smell. It was like flute music, but also like a firework display, and the smell of flowers and rain. The song just came straight into his head. He wasn't hearing it with his ears. It was like a dream. The song had no words, it just had tunes, feelings, colours, smells, tastes. It was beautiful, but it was also sad in places. There were brightly coloured patches of happiness and the taste of apple, and then deep blue and purple sadness which smelled like wet roads in summer. Then a feeling of gladness, and the smell of freshly cut grass and the taste of cake.

Brian began to dream. Slowly, the dragon's strange song changed and began to make different shapes in his mind. Weird shapes at first, but then they started to look like real things. He could see sunshine; he could feel cool wind. He could smell mud and grass and trees. Then he felt there was something near him... an animal. More than one, in fact. Something fat and round and pink. He thought it might be other dragons. But they were blurry, and distant. And then the song was over and the strange dream finished. He was sitting in darkness again.

"There are many more songs," said the dragon, and it was only then that Brian realised the dragon's voice came straight into his mind, just like the song had done. And that's how he was speaking to the dragon too: not by using his mouth, but by *thinking*. It seemed so natural and so easy he had not even realised he was doing it, until now.

"Your song made me see things," he told Dragon with his thinking-voice. "It was like being in another place. Did we go to another place?"

"I... don't know. I think so. I could hear someone calling me, like you did."

"I told you before, *you* called *me*!"

"Maybe we called each other. But someone else is calling too. They were in that other place, where my song took us. But I am... too weak to take us there."

"Who was it? Who was calling us?" Brian was desperate to go back there and find out who was calling.

"I don't know."

"And what were those pink things? Were they dragons, like you?"

"No. I don't think there are any other... dragons," the creature said slowly, as if it was trying out the word 'dragon' to see how it felt.

They talked more about what they had seen, and Brian asked the dragon lots of questions, but he didn't know many answers.

Later, Brian said, "I know a song too."

"Then sing it for me," said the dragon.

"Okay." Brian knew he was bad at singing, but somehow he felt that it didn't matter, the dragon would like it anyway. It was his favourite song, it was about a boy who meets a dragon in a cave, just like he had. He forgot some of the words, and he didn't think he got the tune quite right. He could only remember the first two verses. When he'd finished, Dragon said, "That was wonderful. I have never heard anything like it."

"It's my favourite," Brian said. "Miss Neale says it's a sad song, but I can't remember the last bit."

"Who is Miss Neale?"

"She's my teacher."

"Teacher..." said the dragon thoughtfully.

"Yes. She's nice."

"Where does Miss Neale live? Out there? Past the cave?"

"Yes."

"Are there lots of other people like you?"

"Well, I haven't really got any friends."

"Just Miss Neale?"

"Oh, she's not my friend, she's my teacher. Have you got any friends?"

"I did have, but they've all gone now," said the dragon, and Brian suddenly felt a powerful sadness filling him, as if he was sharing the dragon's sorrow.

He found himself breathing deeply, and he wiped a warm tear from his eye. He didn't know what to say. The poor dragon. Alone. How many friends had it once had? Where had they all gone? He knew it wouldn't be right to ask that now though. He wanted to make the dragon feel better, not worse. At last, he said, "Well... I'll be your friend."

"That sounds good," said the dragon.

For a while, they sat there in silence. Even though Brian couldn't see the dragon, or hear it, somehow he could feel it there beside him, and for now, that was enough. But, after a while, Brian started to feel cold. Also, he wasn't sure how long he'd been out, and he was hoping to slip back into the house before Emily and Mark realised he'd gone. "I've got to go home now," he said. "Sorry. I'll come back again though, Dragon." He reached into the darkness and stroked the creature's skin. It was cold and lumpy and smelled of seaweed and sand. Or maybe that was just the smell of the cave. Dragon's strange body seemed to ripple. Brian switched the torch on, but kept the light away from the dragon's eyes.

Brian quickly wriggled between the stalagmites. "Bye, Dragon," he said. As he emerged from the cave a few minutes later, it occurred to him that even Terry didn't have a friend like this. No-one had a friend like Dragon, except the boy in the song, but that was just a story, for children.

Terry

One day, when the sun was shining on the fallen leaves which had begun to gather on the playground, Brian played football with Gary and some of the other kids. Gary was someone everyone liked, even the teachers. He wasn't mean, and he never got into trouble. Gary always brought a football to school, and he sometimes let Brian play, if someone was away and they needed an extra player. But, today, when Brian had tried to score and had missed by a mile, Terry had said to Gary, "What d'you let him play for?" Gary looked as if he didn't know what to say. Brian scowled at Terry and decided he didn't want to play football anymore. He went and sat by the tree and buried himself with leaves. He wondered what Dragon was doing now. But Dragon seemed so far away, it was almost as if he didn't really exist. He wondered if it had all been just a dream.

In the art lesson that afternoon, Terry looked at Brian's picture. He'd finished his colour-wheel, and Miss had said he could paint whatever he wanted now, so he was painting the dragon.

"What's that?" Terry said.

"My friend."

"It's ugly. It must be your girlfriend."

"Get lost."

"Does she stink, like you?" Terry was smiling.

"I don't stink."

"You do."

Miss Neale was looking across at them.

"And you haven't got any friends," Terry whispered. Then he went back to his table.

A bit later, Brian was on his way to the sink with a jar of water in his hands. He passed Terry.

"I have got a friend, actually," Brian said.

"So?" said Terry.

"You haven't got a friend like him. He hates you."

"So? He's ugly, I saw your picture. Looks like an alien."

"He's a dragon and you'll never find him." Brian pushed past Terry as he headed off towards the sink. Terry followed him.

"Aaahhh, does wittle Bwian still believe in dwagons?" mocked Terry.

"He's real, but you'll never see him."

"Why are you lying?"

"I am not lying."

"Yes you are, liar. Just because you've got no real friends. Who'd want to be friends with a dragon anyway? It'll probably eat you."

"He won't," Brian said, emptying the water into

the sink.

"It will, then it'll be sick and throw you up!" A girl called Nadia, who had come to get some more water, giggled. "It'll throw you up," went on Terry, "or it would get indigestion, and you'd have to call the vet. 'Cept it's eaten you so you can't. Then it would lie down and die. And that would be the end of the dragon. And you!" Nadia laughed at Terry's idea.

"There *is* a dragon," Brian shouted, "and he's going to kill you!" He pushed Terry so hard that he stumbled backwards into Roger, who, as usual, began to cry. Terry looked really angry. "Don't push me," he said, and shoved Brian back. Brian slipped, and the jam jar he was still holding smashed in the sink. Miss was already storming over. She moved Roger out of the way and ordered everyone away from the sink.

"What on Earth were you doing?" she demanded, her voice filled with disbelief rather than anger. The whole class had stopped and was listening now. "Right, no more painting for either of you."

Terry said, "But *he* started it!"

"Did *not*!" Brian said. He was so angry he felt as if he was going to cry. He hated Terry.

They spent the rest of the day glaring at each other across the room, while everyone else painted. At the end of the day, as Brian met Emily at the gate, Terry and Gary walked past. Terry stopped. He looked at Brian, then at Emily and her friends.

"Oh," said Terry, "that's the dragon." Terry turned and ran, and after a moment, Gary followed.

The Old Woman and the Pigs

It was a Saturday afternoon, and Brian felt all drowsy. All he wanted to do was go and see Dragon, but it was raining, and it seemed like such a long way today, so he just sat on the sofa and drew.

Emily was upstairs, sorting out her wardrobe.

Brian drew a picture of Dragon, using the colouring pencils Emily had got him for his birthday, which was yesterday. She'd got him a few other things too, clothes mostly, and a new pair of school shoes. Dad had got him some books to read, but they were quite hard and really boring, and they didn't have any pictures in at all.

It was hard to draw Dragon because he still didn't really know what Dragon looked like, even though he'd seen him loads of times now. He knew he had big eyes which took up most of his head. And he knew his skin was soft and wrinkly and white. But even with the torch, it was hard to see Dragon. He couldn't shine it straight on him because it hurt his eyes, so most of the time Brian only saw bits of him. He sometimes kept the torch switched on, but the light only seemed to fill dragon's alcove with deep, black shadows which wrapped him up as if in a blanket so Brian still couldn't see him properly. Brian knew the creature didn't really look like a dragon, and he was too small to be one. Maybe he wasn't really a dragon at all; it didn't really matter.

Brian drew Dragon's eyes, and a long shape for his body. He drew himself next to Dragon, and trees around them. He'd made the trees wobbly, like in a dream, because that's what the trees were like in Dragon's song.

And then Mark came in.

"Hello, Bri," he said.

"Alright."

"What're you drawing?"

"Nothing."

"Let's see." He bent over and looked at the picture. "Nice," he said. "What's that?"

"That's Dragon."

"Oh. Cool!"

"He's not like other dragons," Brian said. "He's small, and he doesn't have a tail. And I don't think he breathes fire."

"Are you sure it's a dragon then? Looks more like a caterpillar or something."

"It's Dragon."

"You've got one hell of an imagination, mate."

"It's not my imagination. Dragon's real."

"Really? Fantastic!" he said. "Where's Em then?"

"Upstairs," Brian said.

"Cool. See you later, Bri," Mark said, and then in a deep and important sounding voice, added, "Sir Brian, Friend of Dragons!" And he saluted him. Brian saluted back and smiled, and Mark went bounding up the stairs.

A little bit later, the rain eased off, and Brian decided to go out to see Dragon after all. He wasn't grounded anymore, so he went and told Emily and Mark he was going out.

"Alright," Emily said, "but make sure you're back by tea time. And don't go far."

*

Whenever Brian visited Dragon, they always talked about things. Nothing much, just Brian's life. Dragon wanted to know everything. Brian told him over and over again about Emily and Mark and school and Terry. Dragon seemed to love just listening. Brian even told him when he had been in trouble at school sometimes. Dragon said Terry sounded mean.

Then Dragon would start to sing his song. Soon, the sounds would start to form shapes and smells and feelings, and it would stop being like a song and start being like a place. There was the smell of the forest, and of the sea. There was the smell of summer.

It seemed like a dream at first, as it usually did, but today it began to seem much more real, and

Brian felt as if he was actually there. The pictures were clearer than ever. So were the smells and feelings and sounds. He could see the trees. He could see their leaves and the twigs, and hear the hiss of the breeze passing through them, and smell the damp undergrowth. Looking down, he could see the grass and the stones and around him and he could see bushes and bracken.

He couldn't see himself though. He couldn't see his own legs or body or hands. He was invisible. He felt as if he was floating in the air.

Dragon was beside him. He couldn't see him, but he knew he was there. It was as though they had left their bodies behind and floated away to another land. It seemed so real now, not like a dream or like images created by the music. They *really were there*, like ghosts, in that bright, sunny forest.

Brian found he could move about. It wasn't like walking, it was as if his thoughts made him move. He could float to where he wanted to go. He could go fast or slow, forwards or backwards. It was an amazing feeling. He had no body, no arms, no legs, and he felt free. He laughed, and made himself float around the trees. He wasn't very good at it at first, and he kept going right through them. When he did that, everything went black for a second, and he felt a strange flash of warmth, until he came out the other side. He was excited and happy and free. This was real, and there was nothing bad here, and he was with his friend, the dragon.

There was a noise ahead of them, a voice, and the sound of some animals. Then, as they went round a bend in the path, they saw an old woman, stooping, and carrying a basket which looked heavy. With her, to Brian's amazement, were three fat and slightly hairy pigs. Brian realised they were the pink things he had seen so many times before, inside Dragon's songs.

Excitedly, he began to go towards them. He called to them. "Piggies! Hello, pigs!"

"I don't think they can hear you," said Dragon, "I don't think they know you're here."

But Brian went speeding over to them. He reached out to stroke the pigs with his invisible hand. At least, it felt as if he was reaching out, but he couldn't see his hand, and he couldn't feel the pigs. He knew what pigs felt like because his class had been on a trip to a farm. They feel rough, and their hair is spiky, and he could see these pigs would be like that too, but he couldn't feel anything except that they were warm.

The pigs walked with the old woman, snorting and sniffing the ground. Sometimes they bumped into each other and sniffed each other's ears. Then they hurried to catch the old woman up. One of them was slightly smaller, and seemed playful and excited. Brian was desperate to stroke them and play with them, but they didn't even know he was there.

The old woman was further down the path now. The pigs' fat bottoms wiggled as they walked.

"Come on, Dragon," he said, his heart beating faster with the excitement and frustration, and he hurried after them. Dragon was with him.

The woman and the pigs walked for a while. Soon, they turned away from the path, and stepped over a little ditch. Then they went along a narrow track through brambly undergrowth, into the forest. In places, the undergrowth was so thick there hardly seemed to be any path at all. Brian wondered where the woman was going, and what she was going to do. She kept stopping and picking things out of the grass and putting them in her basket: mushrooms.

And after a little while, she arrived in a wide, sunny clearing. She made her way across the lumpy grass towards a huge old tree which rose from a thick mass of tall bushes and ivy. As she reached the bushes, the old woman pulled back some sort of brown sheet revealing a dark space amongst the foliage, ducked her head and disappeared inside.

"Where did she go?" Brian gasped, speeding after her, past the pigs which were now sniffing about and playing in the grass. And it was only then that he saw there was more than just bushes around the base of the tree. Built round the tree's wide trunk was a little house made of wood and mud, partly covered in ivy, and in other places leafy, grassy plants sprouted from it in thick clumps. Its roof was covered in long grass and tangled plants, and the bushes surrounded it so it could hardly be seen. The brown sheet, Brian now saw, was an animal skin, and it was the front door of the old woman's house. Brian felt like laughing, but in his amazement he could hardly even breathe. This house was like something from a story book, and he was enchanted.

"Wow!" he said. "I wish I lived here!" and he went inside, through the animal skin doorway, even though he could just as easily have passed straight through the wall. Dragon followed him. It was very dark inside, and hot, and it smelt strongly of mud and smoke and wet grass. The wide tree trunk around which the house was built was hollow, creating a tiny room in the middle of the house, all craggy like his cave. There were hundreds of plants and things hanging up inside it, and there was a strange little bed in there too which curled round the inside of the tree. Brian, lost in curiosity and delight, saw that the rest of the house was wrapped all round the tree's outside in one big, ring shaped room. As he crept through it, he saw clumps of flowers and dried plants hanging on the walls, and there was even a little doll made of straw. Brian *loved* it.

The old woman was sitting on a stump of wood, with a wooden plate on her lap, chopping up some vegetables. They looked like potatoes, but they were very muddy. She didn't seem to know Brian and Dragon were there.

Brian moved towards her. He looked closely at her hair. It was silvery in places, and black in others. He looked at her dark eyes, and wondered why they didn't both look quite in the same direction. He looked at the lines round her eyes, and the cracks in her lips. He looked at her thin nose, and the big wart on it. Or maybe it was a mole. He looked at the fingers which shook as they sliced the vegetables. He wondered if she was a witch. He didn't think she was an evil one though because of the gentle way she had spoken to her pigs, and patted their heads.

"Hello," he said. The woman didn't reply, or blink, or even seem to hear him. She got up and scraped the vegetables into a round, black pot which she heaved up onto a stove. It was a very small stove, but was a proper, black metal one like in an old house. The fire inside it shone orange through the slits in the door, and filled the room with its warm glow. There was even a metal chimney that went out through the mud wall. As the old woman moved about, Brian smelled her sweat and her hot breath.

"She's real though, isn't she?" he said, remembering that this adventure had started as one of Dragon's songs.

"She's real," said Dragon thoughtfully. "She's a real person. She came into the cave for a while, a long time ago."

"Really? She came to the cave?"

"The pigs weren't with her. And she was frightened. I think she was in danger. She called, but I was not properly awake. I don't think I was even properly alive." Brian didn't know what that meant, but he was too absorbed in looking around this strange, cluttered place to ask. "I saw her, but it was as if I dreamed her. Something terrible had happened to her..."

"Really?" Brian said. "What had happened to her?"

Dragon didn't answer.

"Well, I think she's alright now," Brian said, "in her little house."

"But... It's so long since I've done this you know, so long. I don't even know why we've come here. I don't know *how* I do this. I've forgotten so much. But I think... I think something bad might be going to happen to her, and we might be able to help."

"You mean, *another* bad thing? Like when she came to the cave?"

"Maybe," Dragon said after a long pause.

"She looks sad, doesn't she?" Brian said.

The old woman stopped.

It was as if she was listening for something.

Brian wondered what it could be. He listened too. What had she heard? He could hear nothing, just the fire, and the wind in the trees, and the pigs outside snorting at the doorway.

She shook her head, muttered something, and carried on with her cooking. She threw some scraps of vegetables out of the door. The pigs snaffled them up and poked their noses into the house.

"Hello," Brian said to the pigs, even though he knew they couldn't hear him.

Again, the old woman looked around, her grubby forehead creased. She moved towards Brian. He could feel Dragon right beside him.

"She can hear you," Dragon said, surprised.

"Can she?" Brian said excitedly. "How come? She couldn't before." But without even waiting for Dragon to explain, he said to the old woman, "My name's Brian! Hello!"

The old woman looked as though she was going to faint. She put her hand on her forehead, staggered backwards, and she grabbed some kind of plant from where it was hanging above her bed inside the hollow tree trunk. She moved it in the shape of a cross in front of her body, and then held it out at arm's length towards where Brian and Dragon were. Brian thought she was trying to give it to them at first, but he saw her hands were shaking.

"What's that?" he asked her.

"I think she's scared of us," Dragon whispered.

Brian moved towards her. "Can I play with your pigs?" he said, excited about having new friends.

The old woman's arm fell to her side, and the flowers fell to the floor, and she sat down on the little stump of wood which was her only chair.

"My name's Brian. What's yours? I haven't got many friends. Have you?" She shook her head slowly. "'Cept Mark. He's my friend. He's got a motorbike. And a jacket with pictures on."

She was shaking her head a bit. "Mark," she whispered.

"He's my friend. I like Gary too, but Mark's my favourite. I'm Brian."

"Brian," said the old woman.

"I love your house," Brian said. "It's really nice here, isn't it Dragon?"

The old woman jumped up and held the flowers forward again. "Dragon... Where? Dragons're wicked creatures!"

"This one's not," Brian said quickly. "He's friendly, aren't you, Dragon? He's my friend."

"Hello," Dragon said, uncertainly.

The woman lowered the flowers again. "Where

are you?" she said. Her accent was strange and her voice was croaky. "I can't see you."

"That's because we're not really here, because... I don't know why really. Ask Dragon."

Still shaking, she waved the flowers in the air and said, "D... Dragon, why... why can't I see you?"

"Well," Dragon said. "That's because I... I am too weak to make you see us, but I am getting stronger because you can hear us now. I'm quite old you see, and I have forgotten a lot, but I am learning again, I am getting stronger, and I am starting to remember."

The old woman began to mumble, looking about in the air all over the place. Then she said, "But... who are you? You sound like children. Are you ghosts?"

"Not ghosts. I'm Brian. And he's Dragon."

The woman put the flowers down again, and she seemed to be starting to smile. "You don't seem like wicked spirits, or demons," she said. "Or dragons."

"What's a demon?" Dragon whispered to Brian.

"I don't know, but there's a boy called Damon in my class."

Just then, one of the pigs poked its nose inside the hut. The woman stroked its head and patted its back. "Now then, Mary," she said to her pig, "What do you think? You can tell me if they's good or not." Brian began to chuckle at her strange, curling accent and sing-song tone. "Oi," she said. "What are you laughing about? I ain't said nothing funny!"

"Your voice, it sounds funny!" Then he realised that was probably rude and he stopped laughing. "Sorry."

"I just talk normal. It's everyone else who's strange," she said. "Mary here don't think I'm strange," she said cuddling the pig. Then she sat up as if she'd just realised something. "What am I doing?" she cried out sharply. "What am I doing? I'm talking to spirits! I must have finally gone doolally! I've lost possession of my faculties, Mary!"

"Mary?" Brian said.

"It's a good name for a pig," the woman said after letting out a long sigh. She didn't look so scared anymore. The pig, Mary, was looking about in the air now.

And then another pig tried to squeeze inside past her.

"Well I never," the woman said, shaking her head. "They can hear you too! I was thinking you must just be in my head, but if they can hear you... Well, they ain't scared of you. They'd know if you was evil. Animals can tell things like that. 'Specially pigs." She shooed the pigs outside again. "There ain't room in here for myself," she said, "let alone pigs and dragons. Now get out all of you!" Then she went out too. Dragon and Brian followed them into the sunshine. The pigs trotted around sniffing things, running a bit, and bumping into each other, snorting and grunting. The old woman played with them. She chased them, and mimicked their noises. They seemed to love her, and always wanted to be near her. They ran away when she chased them, but they always came back to her again. She sat down in the grass and rolled around and the pigs sniffed her face and licked her.

Then she sat up. She rubbed the pigs' bellies.

"You still there, you demons?" she called.

"Yes," Brian said.

"Well, let me tell you about my pigs. They seems to trust you, so you must be good demons. This here, who you've met, is Mary. Fat ain't she?" She wobbled Mary's belly. "Was a runt. Can you believe it?"

"What's a runt?"

"A runt's the tiniest one of the litter that farmers don't want cos they never grow big and strong enough to be any good to sell." Brian was still confused. He thought litter was crisp packets and rubbish in the playground, but he knew that wasn't what she meant. "Ha! Look at her now! This ole farmer I knew, he was about to kill 'er. I met him, just by chance, at the river. He was going to drown her! I convinced him to let me have her, and she grew up big and strong, didn't she. Strong as any pig and not runty at all. She used to have a husband," she said, stroking Mary's back as if consoling her, "called Joseph. See? Mary and Joseph, like in the Bible. Got Joseph from a fair. Wanted company for Mary, see. He was a runt too. They was going to kill 'im. 'Put him out of his misery,' the man said to me in his hoity-toity accent, so I rescued him. About five years ago, that was, and he grew up fit as a fiddle, but..." She seemed to gaze right through Brian, at distant, painful memories. "Poor old Joseph," she said, and Brian realised she was telling him Joseph had died. Brian wondered if he should say something to make her feel better, but, perking up, she quickly went on, "And this one, she's Jesus." She laughed a bit. "I know she's a girl, and Jesus was a boy, but, she's the child of Mary and Joseph, so what else could I call her?" She laughed again, and Brian did too. "I had to sell the rest of the litter of course, but I kept her cos she had these dark, imploring eyes. I just couldn't part with her. And this one too; he's Beelzebub." She laughed louder than ever now, snorting like the pigs. "Beelzebub's the only name I had left," she said. "Jesus didn't have a brother, well, some folks say he did but I don't think so, so I named him after the devil instead! He ain't no devil really, but it does me good to remember that the devil himself is never far away, and Beelzebub is a constant reminder of that fact."

"What's a litter?" Brian said. His head was full of questions and he didn't wait for an answer before he asked his next one. "Why did you say the Devil is called Beeli—Beelizi—"

"Beelzebub? Ain't you never heard that before?"

"No. I just thought he was called The Devil."

"Oh, well that's good," said the woman. "If you don't know his name then you ain't in league with him."

"What's that mean?"

"It means you ain't evil, like the devil," she said. "You ain't working for him."

"Well, I do get into trouble at school sometimes."

"School? Do demons go to school then? No, don't tell me about that. This is all too much!" And she shrieked with wild laughter. "I haven't even told you my name! I'm Isabelle."

"Isabelle," Brian said.

"Isabelle," said Dragon, who had been alongside Brian the whole time.

"Yes, that's me name, don't go and wear it out now." And she pretended to shake hands with her new demon friends.

They stayed with Isabelle and her pigs all afternoon. They watched them walk about in the woods and play, and Isabelle told them lots of things about the trees and flowers, and how to make medicines from them, and how to cook with them, and what you could eat and what was poisonous. Brian liked talking to her, and asked her loads of questions which she answered in her funny way. Brian could feel the sunshine, and he completely forgot that really his body was in the cold cave.

"This is amazing," Brian said. "This is the best birthday party ever!"

"Birthday party?" Isabelle said.

"It was my birthday yesterday, but I didn't have a party. This can be my party instead!"

"So now demons have birthdays as well?" Isabelle said. "Well I never," and she chuckled merrily. Then she decided to dance, skipping around Brian, pretending to hold his hands, as if he was her dance-partner, and they both laughed raucously. "Look at me!" Isabelle cried, "I'm dancing with a spirit!" Then she glanced around her. "Shouldn't say things like that too loud," she said more levelly. "People will think I'm mad. Maybe I am!" and she shrieked with laughter again.

Dragon remained quiet, until a lot later.

"I think we are going now," he said eventually. Suddenly, everything seemed to be fading away and Brian was starting to feel cold. Isabelle's voice had already become a distant sound, and the forest looked dim. Isabelle said, "Will you be back?"

"I hope so," Dragon called. Soon, the woods, the

pigs, Isabelle, the smell of smoke and trees, had gone.

It was silent, dark and cold in the cave. There was just the sound of water dripping somewhere and a hiss of waves, or wind.

"We will go there again, won't we?" Brian said, and his voice echoed around the cavern.

"I think so. We have to. We went there for a reason."

"Did we? Why?"

"I don't know that yet. But she was calling me. The..." Dragon's next word was long and musical and full of sounds Brian had never heard before. It was beautiful, and tangled, and it reminded him of the patterns on the tunnel wall. But he didn't know what it meant. Dragon paused, realising Brian hadn't understood. So, Dragon showed him what the word meant by thinking the meaning straight into Brian's mind. It was a thing, something which helped Dragon, something which guided him to the people he could connect with, people like himself and Isabelle. There was no word for it in Brian's mind, and the idea confused him, but he realised the thing Dragon was talking about was in here, in the cavern somewhere. It wasn't alive, and it wasn't a machine either, and it had kept Dragon alive all this time, like magic. And so that became the word they used. "The Magic," Dragon said, "it wanted me to go there, with you. I'd forgotten all about the Magic, but I'm starting to remember now. The Magic guides us, and... and helps us answer the people who call out to us, like you did." Brian didn't bother to remind him it was Dragon who had called him and not the other way round; Dragon always insisted Brian had done the calling and Dragon had answered. It didn't matter. He was here with Dragon and nothing else was important now. "I have seen her in my dreams before," Dragon went on. "One day, she will need us. That's why the Magic connected us to her. I can't go there on my own, though. Maybe when I'm stronger I'll be able to. I am getting stronger. That's why she could hear us today. But with you... your mind is strong, and you help me to get there easily. Maybe that's why the Magic connected you and me too."

Brian glowed with pride and excitement. The Magic, whatever it was, had brought him here to help Dragon! Could that be true? Dragon didn't seem certain, but Brian hoped he was right. But then, he didn't feel as if he'd been brought here by the Magic, he'd just come following the sound of Dragon's voice. And then something else struck him: Isabelle was going to need help. What sort of help? In Isabelle's world, there was little Brian could do. He had no hands there, he was just a spirit. He'd never be able to help her with anything, like fixing her roof, or... or... He couldn't think of any other way he and Dragon could help her, but he was suddenly worried he was going to let them both down. He knew he wasn't much good at anything, even in his own world. He tried not to think about it, and that wasn't difficult. Meeting Isabelle and the pigs had filled him with a bubbly joy, and he sat with Dragon for a long while, stroking the creature's soft, wrinkled skin. It was frustrating listening to him trying to remember his past, and what had happened to all the other dragons. At last, Dragon gave up. He sang one of his songs. It was a sad song. It made Brian dream of creatures crying for help. It reminded him of the dolphin on Mark's jacket, swimming in deep blue water, lost and alone. Dragon sang a happier song then, and Brian didn't understand the pictures this one gave him, but he loved the colours.

Soon, he realised he was really hungry. He said goodbye to Dragon, who seemed sleepy now. He squeezed out through the stalagmites and onto the sloping floor of the cavern. He shone the feeble light of the torch on the walls, and looked at the patterns as he went. He shone the torch up in the air, into the darkness above him. He couldn't see anything much, except a few curves and corners of something. There were big things hidden away up there. Maybe the Magic was up there too.

Laura Godley's Perfect White Socks

It was playtime at last. It was cold, but it wasn't raining anymore so the children were allowed outside for the first time in three days. Brian met Gary on the way out.

"Coming to play football, Bri?" asked Gary. It was his ball so he could choose who played.

"Okay," Brian said, uncertainly. Terry and Gary sorted the teams out quickly and soon they were all charging about. Brian tried to keep as far away from the ball as possible because he knew Terry would make the others laugh at him if he messed up a strike or tackle.

But Gary shouted Brian's name and passed the ball to him. There was a gap right in front of Brian, right down to the goal. His heart was pounding. He really wanted to get this right. He *had* to score.

He kicked it as hard as he could. It wasn't a really bad shot, but it hit the bin they were using as one of the goal posts. It bounced away from the goal, and hurtled towards Laura Godley, who was pretty and clever and popular, and who all the boys, including Brian, wanted to go out with. It hit her leg, splattering mud all over her high white sock. She shrieked, and she and all her friends turned and glared at Brian. All the boys on Brian's team looked at him too and began to moan at him. The ones who weren't on his team laughed. Terry laughed loudest. He made a sound that was so loud it must have hurt his throat. It wasn't even a real laugh, but that made the others laugh louder.

"What d'you pass to 'im for?" Michael said to Gary.

"I was right there for you, Gaz," said Sam.

"Yer, Sam would've scored, Gazza. You should have passed to 'im," Richard said.

Brian felt his throat tightening up. He felt as if he was choking. And then, Laura came over and she shouted at him.

"You stupid idiot!" she yelled. "Look at my socks! You should watch where you're kicking. You've ruined these. My mum will make you buy me new ones."

Brian wanted to disappear. He wished he could be with Dragon and Isabelle. He wished the ground would open up underneath him and he would fall down into it and be gone forever. Everyone was looking at him. He was suddenly angry with everyone, especially Laura for shouting at him in front of all the other boys. He pushed her so hard she fell down. Now she was crying, and Brian ran. As he ran, he shouted all the swear words he could think of, and he knew a lot, thanks to Mark and Emily, and his dad.

And he ran straight into the arms of Mr Morgan who was on playground duty.

*

Brian hated standing outside the staffroom, especially when his cheeks were red and muddy so people could see he had been crying. So many people walked past the staffroom, people he didn't want seeing him there. Like Miss Neale. She stopped when she saw him.

"Oh dear Brian," she said. "What's happened this time?"

He didn't reply. He just turned away.

"I'm only trying to help you, Brian," said Miss Neale.

But he still said nothing. Eventually she sighed, ruffled his hair and went into the staffroom.

Brian's stomach was burning, and he hated the whole world. He hated himself. He had let Gary down badly. That made him feel sick. And he had hurt Laura. That made him feel worse. And now he had been rude to Miss Neale. That made him feel stupid and horrible.

He didn't do any work for the rest of the day, and Miss Neale got cross with him. But he pretended he didn't care. He wanted to prove to Laura Godley, and to Terry and Gary and all the others, that he could not be made to work by anyone, that he was strong, and not just a cry-baby. But Laura kept giving him hateful glances, and the others kept looking at him, sniggering.

As he sat there at his desk, he thought about his only real friends. He thought about what they would think of him if they knew what he was really like. Today though, and every day when he was not with them, that world seemed so far away it was almost unreal. Like a dream.

At the end of the day, Miss Neale came over to him.

"Brian," she said with a sigh, "you've had a bad day today haven't you. I think you need to go home and have a nice evening, and we'll start with a clean slate again tomorrow."

As Brian walked across the playground, dragging his bag through puddles, to meet Emily, he thought to himself, "Tonight I will go and see Dragon."

A Stranger on the Beach

Brian let Emily put him to bed early. She liked to do that when Mark came round. Brian made himself stay awake by sitting in the dark and opening his eyes as wide as he could. When he heard Emily and Mark laughing in her room, he got dressed and sneaked downstairs. He put his coat and hat on, and went outside.

It was cold, and he walked quickly, but didn't run.

Soon, he was heading along the tunnel, shining the torch on the patterns. In some places, he thought he could see the shape of an elephant, and in others, a big fish, but he wasn't sure if that really was part of the pattern or just his imagination.

As he went across the floor of the cavern, he stopped in the middle to shine the torch at the roof. There was something up there, he was sure. But his torch wasn't strong enough. One day, he would buy a really powerful torch and find out what was up there. Perhaps it would be something that would help Dragon remember who he was.

He could already hear Dragon's voice in his head, welcoming him. "Hello, Brian," said Dragon, "how are you?"

"Okay," Brian said, but Dragon seemed to know he wasn't.

"Come and join me here," he said. Hearing Dragon's musical voice already made Brian feel a bit better.

He climbed through the stalagmites. It was harder to get through there these days. Probably because he had his big coat on, he thought.

"What has happened?" said Dragon.

"Nothing," Brian said, even though he wanted to tell Dragon about his horrible day.

"I am so glad you are here," Dragon said. "Are you alright, Brian?" Brian knew the horrible feelings from school were still with him, as if they were stuck to him, and Dragon could tell. "You remind me of someone," Dragon said.

That confused Brian. He wasn't sure why at first, but then he said, "You don't know anyone else, do you?" Brian felt suddenly afraid that he wasn't Dragon's only friend, but he tried to ignore that selfish thought.

"Occasionally, I have heard calls. But people don't usually come near enough, or they just haven't got the ability to hear me. Not like you; you were special." Brian smiled, relieved and proud, and then felt guilty for being glad Dragon didn't have other friends. Perhaps he was lonely. Brian had never really considered that. "But there was one, not so long ago. I was still sleeping." Brian knew that 'sleeping' wasn't quite the right word, but the real word was too long and strange for Brian to understand. Dragon had shown him the true meaning though, so he understood now that Dragon hadn't really been asleep, he had been somewhere between life and death. Miss Neale had once told them about seeds that can survive in the ground for thousands of years before growing into corn. Dragon had been like that, for longer than Brian could imagine. He had been waiting to come back to life. "He was very sad, this boy. I saw him in my dreams. He called, and he heard me too—he had that same special ability that you have—but he never came close enough to wake me like you did. I think... he was *scared* of me. He was so much like you, but not like you. He wanted to come into the darkness, but was *afraid*." As Dragon spoke, an image formed in Brian's mind: The beach; the sun shining on the cliffs; a boy, a bit older than himself, sitting on the rocks. "He needed help. He was very unhappy. He knew I was here... But he just wouldn't come near enough to wake me. I could only watch him from the darkness of my sleep." Brian saw the boy turning away and clambering up over the rocks, and for a moment, there was something about him, the way he moved perhaps, that seemed deeply familiar to him. Did he know this person? "And I never saw him again." Dragon finished his story and the image faded.

Brian put his hand on Dragon's soft head. He didn't mind that he smelt funny, and looked like a great big maggot. "I'm your friend, Dragon," he said. "I'll *always* be your friend. That other boy was stupid to go away and leave you. I'll never do that, I promise!"

A Familiar Place in a Different World

Brian hadn't ever even taken much notice of the seasons before. He didn't even really know which one was which. But that year he had noticed autumn changing into winter. He could smell the difference in the air, especially on clear, bright days when it was cold and fresh.

There were three fishing boats in the harbour. He could see the men working onboard. He could hear their voices, their laughter, and he could smell fish. He wondered if they were happy. Adults don't have to worry about things like children do of course. They don't have the problems that children have. Brian wished he was an adult. But then he wondered if he would still be friends with Dragon if he was an adult. It seemed weird, the thought of an adult being friends with a dragon.

Soon, Brian was sitting with Dragon, closing his eyes, and watching the forest appear around him.

Isabelle was on her knees, picking small mushrooms and dropping them in her basket. The three pigs were moving about slowly, shovelling earth and leaves with their snouts and finding tasty morsel underneath. They knew Brian and Dragon had arrived before they'd even said anything, and before Isabelle knew they were there too. The three pigs snorted and grunted and trotted towards them. Isabelle knew they were there then, and they played for a while, chasing the pigs and being chased by them. Brian realised he didn't think of her as an old woman anymore. She looked old, she had grey hair and a wrinkly, brown face, but she was strong and she ran about like a young person.

After a while they stopped playing and followed Isabelle into the house. There was the smell of dinner and smoke, and it was quite dark.

"I'm going into town," said Isabelle. "There's this chap I knows, sells things on the market. Says he wants to buy some of my brews." She pointed at a line of bottles on the floor next to the doorway. "I'm going to take them down and sell him some bottles of the stuff. Reckon he'll give me a good price." She started placing the bottles carefully into a large basket. "Coming?" she said.

Brian and Dragon followed her out of the little house, and off down the forest path. The pigs bounced along, stopping to sniff things, and to nose at each other.

The path went winding through the forest. They could smell the sea, and hear gulls cry. It always seemed to be warm and sunny in Isabelle's world, even now it was winter in Brian's. After a short while they came to a place where the forest got thinner and they were high up on the cliffs. The sun twinkled on the tiny waves below. Isabelle stood there for a while, and Brian wondered why they had stopped.

"Oh, just admiring the view," Isabelle said when he asked her. "It's beautiful ain't it? Don't you love looking at the sea?" Brian had seen the sea almost every day of his life. "Ain't she beautiful, the sea?" Isabelle went on. "So wild, so big, and free. She can be as gentle as a baby when it pleases her, and she can smash whole ships as easy as if they was eggs."

"I've never seen the sea," said Dragon. "I can hear it sometimes, and taste it even, but I've only seen it in dreams."

Isabelle smiled. "I used to come and sit here when I was a girl," she said. "I'd watch merchant ships coming and going, I used to spend hours just watching."

"It's beautiful," Dragon said. "Isn't it, Brian."

"I suppose so," Brian said. He didn't know whether the sea was beautiful or not, but he loved being here, with Isabelle, Dragon and the pigs. He decided he would look at the sea more often from now on. It would make him think of being here, with his friends, where everything was perfect.

Then Isabelle said, "Well, on we go."

The path twisted its way along the cliff tops,

sometimes heading away from the edge and into the forest for a little while. Even when the sea was out of sight, Brian could smell it and hear it. And the gulls were always circling playfully above them.

Then the path joined a wide, stony track, with deep ruts all along it like car tyre tracks. But they weren't made by car tyres, they were too narrow, and there was no sign of the patterns car tyres made in the mud. Isabelle stumbled in one of them. "Blooming carts," she said, "coming up and down here making perfectly good paths into dangerous places for the likes of me."

The stony track began to slope downwards between the cliffs, towards the sea. It seemed familiar. As it got steeper, and the cliffs got higher around it, Brian began to realise that this place was like the steep road down into the harbour in his own town. This road was just a muddy track, but it was very much like the road he ran down on his way to see Dragon.

Isabelle began to moan. "Oh, it's too steep for my old legs, I'll have to sit down a while." She sat on the gravel and rubbed her knees. Mary came over to her and sniffed. Isabelle scratched the pig's back.

"Dragon," Brian said. "This place..."

"Yes?"

"I... it's like where I live, but different."

"Different?"

"Well, it's like my road, but my road's made with hard black stuff. And there should be a town at the top, and a night club, and some shops, and a big road, and my house and my school, but they're not there because that's where the woods are."

"Oh," Dragon said. "Are you sure it's not the place you know?"

" I... I don't know. It can't be."

Isabelle stood again. "Right now, my lovelies," she said to her legs, "you be good legs and carry old Isabelle to the town now." Brian laughed. She picked up the basket. It looked heavy and he'd have carried it for her if he could.

The road became even steeper, and then he saw some buildings. Cottages with wobbly roofs, like in his own town. And there was the stone harbour wall which curved round the bay. They could see the pub where his dad liked to go, and the shops that Brian knew so well.

Only they weren't shops here, they were houses. There was the mini market, or at least, the building which was the mini market in Brian's town, but here it was just a house, with curtains, and a front door.

There was a boat in the harbour. It was not like any boat Brian had seen in the harbour of his own world. This was a big, dark, wooden boat with two tall masts, and sails all rolled up, and a huge chain coming out of its side, and some thick ropes tying it to the harbour wall. Men were unloading boxes from the boat and putting them onto a cart. A big horse stood there patiently, its skin glistening. The whole place smelt of fish, of the sea and of the smoke that came curling out of the chimneys.

The track they had come down stopped in front of the pub. The area around the harbour was cobbled, including the area that was the car park in Brian's town.

Isabelle was marching towards the pub. Brian and Dragon followed her. Brian noticed the sign above the door. It was a picture of a ship in a bad storm. It was painted on some cracked wood, and the paint was flaking a bit. The pub in Brian's town had a colourful, shiny picture of a smiling sailor with a large tattoo on his arm. Brian was totally confused. Was this his town or not?

Isabelle knocked hard on the door. There was a little window in the door, with black bars across it. After a little while, a face appeared there.

"Yes?" The man was ugly. He had a huge red nose, and lots of deep, dark lines on his pale face. His voice was rough sounding, as if he needed to clear his throat.

"It's me, Isabelle."

"Who?"

"Don't muck around, Jim. I've come with the potions you asked for. Like we arranged. Let us in, for Heaven's sake."

The door opened with a loud creaking noise, and the man, who looked even older than Isabelle, let her inside. He looked at the pigs and made a grumbling noise. Isabelle told the pigs to stay, as if they were dogs, and they did.

"I'll only be a mo'," she said, and patted their heads. Then she said, towards her two invisible friends, "You two, keep an eye on them for me. Or come in with me if you likes." The old man looked at her, confused.

"You oughtn't to do that sort of thing, Isabelle," he said. "You know what people thinks of you."

"Yes Jim, I know. I was only joking," she explained.

"Well, some folks don't find that sort of thing funny," Jim grumbled as he turned away, and Isabelle winked at Brian, which made him want to laugh. She followed Jim inside, and put her basket on a table. Brian went in with her, and Dragon stayed outside with the pigs. Brian wanted to see inside this place. Would it be the same as the pub in his world? He'd only been in there a few times, but he could see straight away that this was not the same place. It was very dark. The small windows didn't let in much daylight, and there were no ceiling lights, only little candles on the table and the bar. The fire at one end gave the room the same sort of orangey glow as in Isabelle's house, and made the air smoky. The floor wasn't covered in carpet, but in straw. And the walls were just lumpy stone painted white. The place was full of a mixture of smells, some sweet, some bitter.

"Now, show us these 'ere bottles," said Jim, sitting on a small stool. Isabelle sat too. She took a bottle and handed it to Jim.

"It's a remedy for a cough," she said. "Secret recipe, but it works." Jim removed the small cork and sniffed.

"Cor blimey," he said with a splutter, "stuff burns just to sniff it." Brian caught a whiff of it too. It reminded him of his dad's breath when he'd been to the pub. "Who'd want to drink the bloomin' stuff?" Jim exclaimed.

"Someone who's got a cough," Isabelle smiled.

"They all for coughs?" he asked.

"Most, except these." She passed him three or four smaller bottles. "They're for a bad head."

Jim looked thoughtful. With his eyes screwed up he looked closely at the bottles, sniffed, and scratched his chin. At last he said, "I'll take half of 'em, see if they sell. I'll have the rest if they do, won't if they don't."

"They'll sell alright Jim, my friend, once word gets round that they really works. People may not like a strange old bird like me, but you know as well as I do they loves my medicines."

Jim got up and rubbed his back.

"I got one for that an' all," said Isabelle. "I'll bring it down next time."

Jim smiled. He disappeared into a back room for a minute, and came back with two heavy, black pots. They clanged like bells when they bumped together on the table.

"I'll give you these now," he said, "and you can have the big one when I see you next, if the stuff sells like you say."

"Awe, Jim," Isabelle said, "this ain't what we agreed, is it? It ain't worth my while if this is all I get. Three pots you said, and the rum."

"But I wants to see 'ow the stuff sells," said Jim. "If it don't sell then it ain't worth *my* while."

"Well," Isabelle went on, "what if I throw in that balm for your back?"

"Ooh," said Jim. He rubbed his back again. "Would you, Iz? It ain't half hurting."

"Ah but you see, Jim," she said, "I needs rum for that, else I can't make it. I can wait for the pot, but I'll be needing the rum." Brian smiled at Isabelle's cleverness.

Jim thought for a bit longer, still rubbing his back, his face scrunched up in discomfort.

"You never mentioned rum just now when you said you'd bring some down next time," Jim said, but Isabelle just sat patiently, without speaking. At last Jim sighed. He stood and went over to the long table. Brian realised that the table, which was really just a few planks of wood on top of empty barrels, was the bar, where people like his dad would buy their drinks. All the drinks were in bottles on shelves behind it. There were some bigger barrels all stacked up on their sides too. They probably had beer in them.

Jim took a bottle from the shelf. He was old and stiff, and could only move slowly. He went to give the bottle to Isabelle, but then held it back as if he was teasing her.

"No extra charge for the back balm then, Isabelle?" he said.

"You drive a hard bargain, Jim my friend," Isabelle said, and smiled. "No extra charge. But don't forget you still owes me a pot."

"And you owes me some back balm."

Isabelle unloaded half of the bottles from the basket as they'd agreed. She stacked the heavy pots Jim had given her together, one inside the other, and fitted them into the basket. They looked even heavier than the bottles, but Brian couldn't help her.

She shook hands with Jim, and he went with her to the door.

After the gloom of the pub, it seemed bright outside, even though they were in the cool shadow of the cliffs. The men who had been stacking the crates onto the cart had stopped their work now and were looking over at Isabelle and the pigs.

"Best go, Isabelle," said Jim.

"Thanks, Jim." Isabelle smiled. Jim quickly went inside his pub and closed the door.

One of the men was coming over.

"They've been watching us for ages," said Dragon. "What do they want, Isabelle?"

"Oh, don't mind them," she said. "They's just nasty men. Come on, pigs." She headed along the track, away from the harbour.

"Oi!" The man waved a fist as he shouted.

"Ignore them," whispered Isabelle.

"Oi! Pig woman! What you doing down 'ere then?" The man had jogged up to them now.

"Go away," said Isabelle, calmly.

"Old Jim don't want you coming down 'ere, pig woman." Brian felt his stomach beginning to ache, just like at school when Terry made fun of him. He wondered what Isabelle would do.

She kept on walking. The three pigs were snorting and grunting.

"He don't like you coming 'ere and giving his pub a bad name."

Isabelle said, "I heard that potion did wonders for your wife's cough though."

The man looked surprised. "Who told you that? I

don't have no need of your potions, witch. No-one does. We don't want to see you 'ere, understand?"

"They might not want to see me, but they'd miss my medicines."

"Go back to your hole, pig woman." To Brian's horror, the man kicked Mary in the side. Mary squealed. Then she turned and bit the man hard on the leg. He shouted in pain and shock, and then kicked out again. He missed this time though, and all three pigs calmly trotted away from him, snorting.

"Look what your damn pig done," shouted the man. He rubbed his leg, and lifted his trousers to show Isabelle the big red mark Mary had made. Isabelle was acting as though the man hadn't even bothered her. "Damn creature bit me!" shouted the man angrily. "Look!"

"Oh dear," smiled Isabelle. "I got some ointment for that." She winked at him and carried on walking up the hill. Brian turned round and saw the other men standing by the cart, laughing unsupportively at their foolish friend.

"We don't want your type down 'ere," called the man as Isabelle began to climb the steep road out of town. Brian watched him limping crossly back to the cart.

"I always gets a bit of that when I come down here," said Isabelle, "but I ain't scared of idiots like him."

"Is Mary alright?" Brian asked.

It was Dragon who replied. "She's not injured," he said. "She's angry though."

Isabelle laughed. "Seems you knows my pigs better'n I know them myself!" She rubbed Mary's side and patted her back. "She's a tough pig, this one. Them men though, they're fools. My brews really do help. But some of them think it's magic, and that makes 'em scared. I can't win: if my brews didn't work, no-one would buy 'em. If they do, they say I'm a witch. Maybe I am, I don't know. But I'm not a bad one. See, I've always been good with herbs. It ain't magic. Mind you, there is magic in that forest, but it's nothing to do with me." She began to whisper now. "There's these stones I find sometimes. They's blue and they glow at night, just a little. You can tell they're powerful as soon as you touch them. Sometimes they calls to me, like a tiny singing voice only I can hear. That's how I find them. I've got a few now, in bottles."

Brian could tell Dragon was thinking about the stones.

"Do you have any with you, Isabelle? I'd like to see one."

"I do," she said. She glanced around to make sure they were alone on the road. Then, she rummaged amongst the herbs in the leather pouch at her belt, and produced a small, bright blue stone. She held it towards Dragon who went very quiet for a while. Brian looked too. It was beautiful: so smooth, such a vibrant sky-blue, with tiny veins of a darker colour rippling and curling through it.

"Do you know what it is, Dragon?" Brian asked.

"It... It has stirred a memory... But... it was so long ago. Keep them, Isabelle. They are important, I think."

"See," Isabelle smiled, tucking the stone away. "There's magic in that forest. Blue stones and dragon spirits. My secrets."

Brian laughed. He turned round and looked back down into the harbour. He could see the men by the cart, far away now. The sun twinkled on the waves beyond them and he felt a strange spark of something inside him, a sort of happiness he had never known before meeting Dragon and Isabelle; a feeling which grew each time he came here, a feeling which seemed to come from the sea and the trees and the smell of this world.

Brian the Bully

After lunch, the bell went, and Brian ran with the other children out of the dinner hall and into the icy air. Terry shoved Brian and said, "You're it," and he and Gary charged off across the playground. Brian chased them, dodging round the other children and splashing through puddles of melted frost. He sped past Laura Godley, making sure she saw how fast he could run.

Gary stumbled as he side-stepped round a bin, and Brian headed for him. He cornered him, but Gary ducked past him. Brian reached out for him, but missed, and sped after him again. Terry ran close to Brian, teasing him. Brian reached for him, but carried on chasing Gary. Terry followed, trying to make Brian turn and chase him. Brian laughed. As they got near to Laura, he suddenly turned. Terry tried to dodge out of Brian's way but couldn't and Brian tagged him. Now Brian was running away, making sure he stayed fairly near to Laura, who ignored him completely and went on walking round the playground with her friends.

Terry was close behind him. Brian soared past a little kid, round a netball post, and through the gap between two groups of girls. Heading back across the playground, he saw Roger standing there. He looked excited and scared, and was jigging up and down a bit. Brian didn't know why. Roger was right in his way and he had to swerve round him.

Roger stuck out his hand and it touched Brian's shoulder.

"You're it!" Roger screamed, and ran off. He was squealing, as if he thought Brian was chasing him.

Brian was confused. He stopped running and turned to look at Terry. Terry was laughing, and shouting, "You're it!"

"But..." Brian said.

"I 'ad Roger just a few seconds ago when I was coming after you. Didn't you see?" shouted Terry.

"Is he playing too, then?" Brian said, feeling a bit stupid.

Just then, Gary ran by, really close. So Brian reached out for him, and missed. Roger was standing miles away from Brian, and every time he looked at him, Roger giggled and ran even further away. Brian, trying not to feel angry with Terry, decided to head for Gary. Soon he was speeding about, laughing and shouting.

When the bell went, Brian was still 'it'. Gary came over.

"You're really fast, Bri. You're nearly as fast as me, and I'm pretty fast, aren't I?"

"Yer," said Terry. "That was an excellent game. Let's play again tomorrow."

Roger ran over too. His face was red and he was grinning. "You never got me," he said. "You never got me!"

"Oh," said Terry, "I forgot you were playing, Podger." Roger's face fell.

Brian wanted to join in with Gary and Terry who were always together these days, usually laughing at some shared joke. Brian wanted Gary to think he was funny, like Terry.

So he said to Roger, "Yer, Podger, I thought you were a..." He couldn't think of anything to finish his sentence with, except, "nodger!" Terry laughed anyway, but somehow, Brian felt he was really laughing at him, not Roger. Gary just smiled. And then he patted Roger on the shoulder in a friendly way.

And Brian felt sick about being nasty to Rodger. He thought of Dragon and Isabelle, but they seemed so far away. When he was here in school, it was almost as if Dragon and Isabelle didn't exist.

During Topic that afternoon, Brian sat with Terry and Gary. So far today, Terry had mostly been nice to him, as he sometimes was. Especially when Gary was there. But Brian never really knew if Terry liked him much. He always felt Terry thought he was a bit stupid, even when he was being friendly.

Miss Neale was helping one of the other children with their work when Terry broke off a bit of Brian's rubber and flicked it across the table at Roger.

It bounced on Roger's work. He looked up, unsure of where it had come from.

For that moment, Brian was in a different world. In this world, he and Terry shared a secret, a special joke. He knew Terry had upset Roger, yet in this moment, Brian and Terry understood each other, and they were together, like partners.

It felt good. Brian didn't want that moment to end. He needed Terry to see he was with him, supporting him.

That's why Brian laughed.

"Stop it," Roger whispered, his face going red. Then, when he wasn't looking again, Brian broke a little bit off the rubber, and flicked it at him too.

"Oi!" snapped Roger, a bit louder this time. Terry laughed quietly, and Brian grinned back.

"I'm telling," Roger said. He put his hand up.

Brian glared at him. "If you tell," he said, unable to stop himself now, "I'll get my sister's boyfriend on you," he whispered. "He rides a motorbike." Roger looked frightened, and put his hand down. Brian looked down at his work as Miss came by. He didn't dare look up in case Roger was telling on him. He could see Terry and Gary suddenly working too.

"Oh good," said Miss, "I'm glad to see you're all

getting on with your work here," and she went away again. Brian looked up to make sure she was not watching. Then he broke another piece off the rubber, and flicked it at Roger, who was doing his work again now. Roger looked up.

"Stop it," he said.

"What?" Brian said. Terry was grinning at Brian. "Get on with your work, Podger," Brian whispered.

"Shut up," said Roger. Terry made a sniggering noise, as if he was about to burst out laughing but was trying to be quiet.

"My friend will get you," Brian said, flicking another bit of rubber, then another, and another.

"Shut up, stinky Brian," said Roger.

Terry stopped sniggering. "Oh," he whispered, "did you hear that, Bri?"

Brian was cross now. He knew he had no right to be, but he was. He threw his whole rubber across the table at Roger. It bounced up and hit him in the mouth. Roger let out a cry, and Terry's laugh turned into a hiss as he tried to stifle it. Miss Neale turned. Roger began telling her, through his tears and saliva and snot, what had happened. He was crying, and Brian could see a speck of blood on his lip. Miss Neale turned on Brian and said, "Get out of this room!" She didn't shout, she just said it with anger. Brian felt horrible suddenly, to think that Miss Neale didn't want to have him in her classroom anymore. He pushed his chair back, and walked out, glaring at Roger until he was through the door.

Out in the corridor, Brian felt his insides burning. He screwed his eyes up and wished he could disappear. He had the horrible prickly feeling of being watched, as if Dragon and Isabelle and all the pigs knew exactly what he had done. He could feel their disappointment. He seemed to be drowning in it. He could hardly breathe; it was squeezing his throat and making him feel sick and dizzy.

Miss came out and talked to him in her disappointed voice for ages. It didn't make any difference. He already felt like the most horrible person on Earth. He didn't even hear her words. All the time, he was thinking of Dragon, and of Isabelle. What would they think of the way he had treated Roger? Brian imagined Isabelle and the pigs, living their peaceful, perfect lives in the woods, and thought of how kind she was, and how surprised she would be if she knew what he had done. He was as horrible as the man who had kicked Mary. If Mary was here, she'd probably bite him. Why couldn't he just be like Isabelle: kind and calm and cool? She certainly wouldn't want to be his friend anymore.

That made him feel lonelier than ever, and with Miss Neale glaring down at him so crossly, but he refused to let himself cry. Then, Miss Neale led him back into the classroom and over to Roger, who had red eyes, and was holding to his lip an enormous blue ice pack wrapped in a tea towel. Brian imagined Roger going home, his mum hugging him, Roger telling her about the horrible boy who had thrown a rubber at him. Roger would feel warm and cared for and loved, but he would also dread coming back to school.

"I think Brian would like to say something to you, Roger," Miss Neale said. "Well, Brian?"

Brian could feel Terry looking at him. It was as if Terry's eyes had laser beams coming out of them, burning into Brian's back. But Miss Neale's eyes were burning him too, and the thought of Dragon and Isabelle finding out what he had done was almost enough to choke him. Roger hadn't done anything wrong. He was like a harmless baby animal, always frightened, always wanting its mum, and Brian could hardly believe he'd been so horrible to someone so helpless.

"Sorry," he managed.

"I don't think Roger heard that, Brian."

"I'm sorry," he said, a bit louder.

"Can you say it as though you mean it please Brian?" Brian was sure he must have said it as though he meant it because he really had meant it, but he said it again anyway.

Roger said, "That's alright," and wiped his nose. Then Miss Neale led Brian to a table away from the others and made him sit down with his topic book.

"I'd like this finished by home time please, Brian," she said quietly.

And he was sure he could hear Terry behind him, sniggering.

*

By the end of school, Brian was hot and tired. It had been a horrible day. He wished he could go back and change it. He walked home slowly, a long way behind Emily and her friends.

They were part way home when Gary pulled up beside him on his BMX, his football scarf wrapped around his face.

"A'right Bri?"

"Yer."

"You really got told off, didn't you," he said, loosening the scarf and revealing his grin.

"Yer," Brian said, and looked down at his feet.

"You comin' out tonight then?" asked Gary. "Me an' Terry's going to the park."

"Maybe," Brian said, surprised Gary had asked him. He expected Gary to hate him now. Gary would never have treated Roger like Brian had done today. Even so, Brian said he wasn't sure he would tonight. He really wanted to visit Dragon, though he was scared Dragon would somehow know how cruel he had been to Roger. Gary said, "See ya then," and cycled off.

And Brian wished he was more like Gary.

Isabelle's Secret

As Brian climbed over the rocky spur to his beach, he could already hear Dragon calling him, like a song in his head. It was easy for Dragon to call him now. Sometimes he felt as if he could hear him when he was still walking down the road. But he was worried about seeing Dragon today. He hoped Dragon didn't know he had been horrible to Roger.

It was cold outside, and the cave was even colder, but the tunnels and the cavern seemed comfortably warm.

"Hello," said Dragon cheerfully as Brian approached.

"Hello," Brian said.

"Is something wrong?" Dragon asked.

"No."

Soon they left the cave and went into Isabelle's world. She wasn't in her house, so they went along the cliff path, calling her name. They found her at a place where the woods went down steeply into a little valley with a river at the bottom. Isabelle was kneeling on a cushion, scrubbing something in the pool at the bottom of a small waterfall. She wasn't wearing her usual clothes. She was wearing a long grey dress that looked very old.

"Hello you two," she said, turning away from her washing and smiling towards them even though she couldn't see them.

The pigs were standing in the river, but when they heard Brian and Dragon they came out of the water, snorting excitedly.

"Hello, Mary," said Dragon, "ahh, lovely to see you." Mary sniffed and grunted in reply.

"Hello, Jesus," Brian laughed as the pig nosed at the air where he was. "A'right Beelzebub?" Brian said. Soon they were playing the usual chasing games and Brian forgot his bad feelings for a while. Isabelle left her work and came to play too. She waded into the water, making her dress all wet, and she splashed water over everyone. Brian felt the cold droplets go through the place where his body should be. He could see them coming, and he felt them go through him like icy fireworks. It made him laugh and squeal. He found he could go right in the water, and under the pigs, looking up through the ripples and waves their legs made as they stomped about looking for him. It was so cold, but he laughed as Beelzebub's snout poked down into the water, blowing bubbles and trying to work out where he had gone.

After a while, the pigs got tired of the game. Isabelle put her washing in a big basket, and led them along the rocky valley, heading out towards the sea. Often, Isabelle and the pigs had to go stomping through the shallow water to get round a tree or big rock.

"I usually comes down here once a month to wash all my clothes," Isabelle told them. "Down here I can let the water fall do most of the work for me. Saves me having to bash them on the rock bare handed." Brian wished Emily would only do the washing once a month; he hated having to help her hang it all up.

They followed the river all the way down onto the beach. It grew wide and shallow, and then it ran down to the sea over the shiny rocks.

They walked along the shale at the bottom of the cliffs. They played games, chasing each other to the sea. Isabelle would laugh, and splash them, especially when Dragon had told her what that felt like.

Later, they took a narrow path which wound its way up the steep hillside between thorns and brambles. Isabelle's face was very red by the time they reached the forest above. Mary, Beelzebub and Jesus lay down in the grass, with their tongues out. Brian and Dragon went through the bushes to the edge of the cliff and looked at the sea. Gulls were flying round and round in circles, making their strange crying noises.

"Are they dancing?" Dragon said.

"I don't know," Brian said. "But they always do it."

"Are you both daft?" called Isabelle. "They're just trying to catch fish!"

They went into the woods now, and soon the thin track came out at the main forest path they knew well. They followed that for a little while, then turned off into the bushes towards Isabelle's house.

When they reached the clearing, Isabelle hung the wet clothes and blankets on the bushes. Then she sat down on the grass and the pigs wandered around, sniffing at things.

"Ahh," sighed Isabelle, "we are lucky. We have such beauty all around us. Is it like this in your world Brian?" He looked round at the forest. He liked the way the sun made the leaves glow. He liked the way the trees were all different, leaning one way or another, all tangled and bent. Was that what Isabelle meant? He didn't know if that was beautiful or not, but he liked it. And it certainly wasn't like this in his world.

"Not really," he said. "A bit. My world's horrible sometimes," he said. The sick feeling in his tummy had come back again now. What if Dragon and Isabelle knew what a bad person he was?

"Well," Isabelle said, "what's horrible about it?"

"I haven't got any friends," Brian said. "Sometimes everyone hates me."

"You've said that before," Isabelle said, "and I told you what I think. If I worried when people didn't like me, what would I do? Most people in this world thinks I'm a witch, and they'd think it even more if they heard me chatting with spirits! You've got to learn to like yourself."

Brian thought about that, and then said, "But I don't like myself." He thought about being nasty to Roger, and being rude to Miss Neale, and he thought about the way Emily cried when he got into trouble, and how he pushed her away sometimes when she tried to hug him.

"Now why ever not?" Isabelle said. She sounded surprised. Dragon didn't say anything.

"You'd hate me too, if I told you," Brian said.

"Now, I doubt that, my friend," she said.

"You would."

"I promise, Brian, I won't hate you. I'll bet that it ain't that bad at all."

"I'm horrible," Brian said. Instantly, he wished he hadn't told her that. He didn't even know why he had. He didn't want her to know what he was like. But, for some reason, he had the feeling that he *should* tell her.

"Now," Isabelle responded, "that ain't true or else I wouldn't be your friend."

"Yes I am, I'm horrible to Roger. I made him cry!" Guilt was choking him again. He didn't know what

Isabelle was going to say. He couldn't imagine Isabelle or Dragon ever being unkind to anyone, and he knew he didn't deserve to be their friend.

"Oh dear," said Isabelle. "Tell me, Brian, who's this Roger?"

"He's a boy at school and I made him cry."

"There you go on about school again. I'm sure spirits don't go to school!"

"Well I do." He said it a bit angrily, even though he wasn't cross with Isabelle.

"Now listen," she said, "it ain't unusual for people to be horrible to their friends—"

"He's not my friend."

"Well, sometimes people are horrid to each other. It don't always mean you're a bad person. If you was a bad person, you wouldn't care about what you done, but you do, I can tell. That's cos you're a good person, or were when you were alive."

"I am alive."

"I've done my fair share of being horrible to people," Isabelle said. "I've been rude, I've had fights, I've hurt people. I ain't perfect, nowhere near it neither. No-one is. Probably there ain't a person in the world who ain't never been nasty to someone else. Difference is, some people feel guilty and try not to do it again, like me, and like you. So don't think I might hate you, Brian. I forgive you, as long as you forgive me for the things I've done."

"What things?" Brian said, surprised.

"Well... I was horrible to this little boy in my village when I was a girl, and..." She stopped.

"What happened?" Brian asked.

"The boy ran away. It was my fault. He wasn't a bad lad. Don't even know why I done it. I was mean and horrible to him though. He got hurt, badly. Fell out of a tree into a river. That wasn't what I wanted of course. Was my fault though. I was just showing off to the other children... It makes me feel sick to think of it even today." Brian didn't know what to say. He couldn't imagine Isabelle being nasty to anyone.

"Did he die?" he asked.

"No. Not quite. But he was sick for a very long time because of being in the freezing cold water, and he nearly did die. He was the parson's son, and the parson was also the one who taught the children in the village about letters and numbers. The old fella hated me for what I'd done to his son and never let me forget it. He caned me to within an inch o' death whenever the fancy took him, and he made sure everyone knew what a sinner I was." She paused. "But I *was* a sinner, an' I deserved everything I got. That boy nearly died because o' what I done. It wasn't the caning and the witch-hunts what made me change me ways."

"Witch-hunts?" Brian asked.

"Well, I was good with herbs and medicines so I s'pose that's why the rumours started, but the parson helped them along of course. And I can't say I blame him. He was a holy man, and I had the devil in me."

"You haven't," Brian said.

"Everyone has, Brian, my friend. You just have to get to know it. Some people thinks they don't have one, but them's the worst. The devil does his dirtiest work when he's in someone who don't know he's there." Just then, Beelzebub came nosing up to Isabelle. She laughed. "Beelzebub likes to remind me of that!" she said, slapping his back. Then she was quiet for a short time. Brian hadn't understood all of what she'd said, but somehow she had made him feel better. When he glanced at Isabelle again, her face looked suddenly ancient. He often forgot she was an old woman because she was so energetic and funny, but now her face looked wrinkled and old, and Brian realised it was full of sadness.

Isabelle wiped the corner of her eye. There was a tear there, Brian saw the sun sparkle on it.

"Are you sorry for what you did?" Brian asked.

"More sorry than you'll ever know. I'll never forgive myself," said Isabelle.

Brian thought about that for a moment. He knew how horrible he felt to have made Roger so upset, and he realised Isabelle must feel far worse because the boy she was horrible to had almost died. What if Roger ran away, or climbed a tree to get away from Brian? What if he fell and hurt himself, or worse? Brian would never forgive himself then. He'd hate himself forever. And yet... Isabelle was such a *good* person. She didn't deserve to hate herself forever, did she? He thought about how happy she made him, how he felt warm and safe and contented and excited to be alive whenever he was here with her. No, she shouldn't be sad.

"We forgive you, don't we Dragon," he said.

"We do," Dragon said.

Isabelle sniffed and smiled. "Thank you, my friends. Forgiveness from the spirit world! That's more than I could ever have dreamed of!" Then, she added, dramatically, "And I forgive you too, Spirit Brian, Friend of Dragon." Brian felt as if he was glowing.

"People are strange," Dragon said. "They are like detailed and complex patterns. They are like the forest and the sea."

Brian didn't know what he meant, but he was still thinking about what Isabelle had said, so he didn't ask. Isabelle's story had shocked him. He still loved her of course, despite what she'd done. In fact, somehow he seemed to love her more than ever now. And she still seemed to love him too. Did that mean he wasn't a horrible person after all? As he left the cave and walked back up the cliff road later that evening, towards home, he knew what kind of person he wanted to be. He wanted to be wise, like Isabelle, and he wanted to be kind to people, like Dragon.

But, feeling the real world all around him, thinking about Emily, and school, and Terry, he knew it would not be easy.

Beer and Blood

Gary and Brian sat on Brian's bed and watched the rain running down the window. Brian's raindrop had just beaten Gary's for the third time, but they were bored of that game now. It looked like the thunder storm had finished, but it was still too wet to go outside.

"What shall we do?" said Gary.

"Dunno."

"Surely the rain's gonna to stop soon? Maybe we could go round to Terry's and play on his computer."

"Okay," Brian said, but really he didn't want to. Sometimes Terry, Gary and Brian would play together these days, and everything would be okay. But he preferred it just being himself and Gary. Gary liked doing the things Brian liked to do, like drawing. But they were bored of that today. And now Gary wanted to go to Terry's. Brian wished he could be like Gary, friends with everyone, never having to worry that people would make fun of him, because everyone liked him.

The rain was stopping now, just like Gary had said. "Let's go to Terry's then."

"Alright," Brian said. He picked his coat up off the floor and put it on.

As they went out onto the landing they could hear voices from downstairs. It was Emily's voice, and she sounded angry. She began to shout, and Brian's dad yelled back. Brian and Gary stood there on the landing and listened, but couldn't tell what they were saying from here. Slowly, without looking at Gary, Brian began to creep downstairs.

"Don't talk to me about money, Dad!" yelled Emily, "I do more than you do to keep us in food and clothes—"

"Listen to me!" yelled Dad, and as Brian got to the bottom of the stairs, he saw the two of them in the kitchen. "You never think, do you? 'Course I'm going to talk about money. How the hell are you going to afford to look after it?" Brian looked at Gary. He smiled back, but his face was a bit red. Brian wondered what they were talking about. Perhaps Emily wanted to get a dog.

"Don't speak to me like that!" Emily yelled. "At least I'll be better at it than you ever were!"

"I did everything I ever could for you!" Brian's dad yelled back, and punched the kitchen table, making one of the beer bottles fall over and roll off it, to the floor. Beer spilled out of it, but they both ignored it. "It's not easy looking after two children on your own you know!"

"Yer, you proved that didn't you!" Emily shouted, and without meaning to she stepped forward into the puddle of beer. "You couldn't cope without blowing half the money you earn on drink! No wonder we have to go to school in rags! Don't kid yourself that you ever did anything for us. If it wasn't for me we'd all starve!"

Brian watched his dad's face as Emily spoke: his angry expression, his clenched fists, and he could smell the beer even from here.

But then the expression changed. He suddenly looked dreadfully sad. It reminded him of Isabelle. He unclenched his fists and turned away from Emily.

"I did my best," he said, more calmly now.

But Emily was still really angry. She screamed, "don't turn away from me you drunken old sod!" and she slapped his back with both her hands. Dad turned round to face her again. He opened his mouth to shout at her, but, shocked, she stepped backwards too quickly. Her feet slipped in the puddle of beer and she fell. Two chairs flipped over as she went down, and there was a horrible crack as something hit the hard kitchen floor.

She just lay there, all still. Her eyes were half open.

Brian's dad stood there with his mouth gaping.

Brian ran over to Emily and dropped to the floor

in front of his dad's feet, his knees in the beer-puddle. He gasped when he saw the pool of blood around Emily's face. He pushed the chairs off her and found himself hugging her, shaking her, calling her name.

Emily groaned, blinked, and opened her mouth.

Then she was sick.

The sick spilled out of her mouth, over the side of her face, into the pool of blood. Then she was coughing badly, and choking, but she didn't sit up. It was as if she was asleep, but choking at the same time.

"Dad!" Brian cried, but his dad was backing away.

Brian sobbed as he put his fingers into Emily's mouth. He had no idea what he was doing. He just knew she was choking and he had to get the sick out of her mouth and throat. His tears fell onto her face.

Then Gary was kneeling next to him. He said calmly, "She'll be better on her side. She's choking." Brian just stared at him. Gary's voice was gentle, but it sounded shaky, and his face was white. Together they turned Emily onto her side, away from the mess on the floor. She kept coughing, but not so violently now. "She's breathing," Gary said. And, behind them, there was the sound of Brian's dad crying, struggling for words:

"Hello, ambulance... quick, oh God... please... Yes, my daughter's fallen... Yes, unconscious...

Hurry up will you… oh God…"

With a tea towel, Gary began to wipe the blood and vomit away from Emily's face.

"Got to stop the bleeding, Bri," he said. Brian hadn't even noticed that the pool of blood was getting bigger and all the hair at the back of her head was soaked with it. It seemed to him as if everything had slowed down, like in a film. He hardly even heard Gary's words. But he watched him find a clean bit of the towel. Gary looked closely at her head, and moved her hair with his fingers. He found the cut and pressed the towel against it. Then he said something to Brian. Brian didn't reply; he hardly even knew Gary had said anything. But Gary shook him, and said it again. "Bri, press this really hard. Keep pressing it, as hard as you can." Brian nodded, and took the towel from him. Gary showed him how to press it against the wound with one hand whilst bracing her head with the other. "Harder," Gary said. "It'll help stop the bleeding. My mum showed me. She's a nurse." So Brian pressed it as hard as he could, and he kept pressing it even when his arms hurt so much they began to shake.

Then his dad knelt beside him and put his hand on Emily's cheek. "Oh, Em," he said. "Em, I didn't mean it…" He kept slowly shaking his head and his face was wet and red. Brian had never seen him look like that. Gary had gone. Brian didn't know where.

Then Dad put his rough hands over Brian's and helped him press the towel.

It seemed as if they were there for ages. Brian's shoulders ached, and the towel was soaked with blood, but all he was aware of was his dad's hand pressing hard against his. Then there was a new sound. It was a loud cry, going up and down like one of Dragon's sad songs...

It was the ambulance siren.

Emily moved. She made a horrible moaning noise, and then coughed.

Then there were other people in the room. They were kneeling beside Brian and his dad, asking what Emily's name was, asking Emily if she could hear them....

It all seemed like a nightmare, as if it wasn't really happening.

Suddenly, Brian was being moved away and guided across the room. He wanted to be sick. He needed the toilet. He felt as if he was falling asleep.

"Hello," said a voice beside him. "My name's Susan, I'm here to help. What's your name?"

Brian looked behind him at Emily but someone else was in the way now, crouching next to her and asking Brian's dad things.

"Hello," the voice beside him said again. "I'm Susan. Can you tell me your name please?" And Brian realised she was talking to him.

"Brian," he said.

"Hello Brian," said Susan. "Is that your sister?"

Behind them, Brian could hear his dad gasping, "Will she be alright? Will she be alright?" whilst the paramedic tried to calm him down and tend to Emily at the same time. Brian wanted to turn and see what was happening, but Susan gently urged him to look at her instead. There was a warmth to her face which soothed him slightly, despite the serious expression she wore.

"Will she be alright?" Brian asked her, and his voice came out like a whisper.

Gary was standing beside him now.

"I should think so," Susan said. "Now, you two, could you just sit over there while we get Emily into the ambulance?"

Gary and Brian sat on the sofa and they watched them putting Emily onto the stretcher, with blankets over her, and straps round her waist and bandages around her head. Brian's dad was standing there, helplessly, shaking his head in disbelief. Emily was moving, groaning, coughing, as the ambulance people swiftly whisked her outside.

Dad followed.

Brian got up to go after him, but Gary said, "Stay here, Bri. Your dad'll be back in minute."

"What's happening?" he managed to say.

"I think they're taking her to the hospital. But

we'll have to stay here. We can't all go in the ambulance." A moment later, the siren whooped into life and the ambulance roared away.

Dad was coming back in the door now. He slowly pushed it closed. Dad kept on staring, as if he could see right through the door and was watching the ambulance disappear into the distance.

He stood there for ages. Brian watched him.

Gary said, "Shall I... um..."

Brian got up.

Gary said, "Would you like me to phone you a taxi, Mr Carpenter? Mr Carpenter?"

Brian looked at Gary. He was white and shaking a bit. Brian knew he should say something to him. Brian knew Gary had been amazing and he should tell him that, but he still couldn't speak. He just couldn't.

He walked past him, and past Dad. He opened the door.

Dad put his hand on Brian's shoulder and said, "Bri..."

Brian let his hand stay there for a few seconds. Then he went out into the cold.

He heard Gary's voice behind him. "Bri, are you okay? Bri?" Brian stopped, but didn't turn round. He couldn't. So he just nodded.

Then he ran.

He had to find Mark.

He heard his dad shouting his name, and he heard him running after him, but he never caught up with him.

Brian knew Mark lived near him. He couldn't remember exactly where though. He ran along the main road. He ran through puddles and splashed icy water all up his legs, but he didn't care. He ran along the road he thought was Mark's, and realised he'd made a mistake. He turned back, and then ran down a different street. That wasn't Mark's road either.

He ran back to the main road, exhausted. He knew he wouldn't find Mark's house so he just walked aimlessly along, trying to get his breath back, the winter air stinging his lungs. He didn't want to go back home. He thought about going to see Dragon, but that seemed all wrong somehow. Dragon couldn't help him now. This was the real world.

Then there was the sound of a motorbike. It sped right past him.

Then it stopped, turned round and came back. The bike skidded to a halt beside him.

The rider took off his helmet hurriedly and shook his long hair out of his face. It was Mark! He looked worried.

"What's happened?" he said, and it seemed as if he already knew something was wrong. "Jesus, I knew it. I just had this feeling... What's happened,

Bri?"

Brian could still hardly speak, but somehow made him understand.

"I knew it," said Mark. "I heard the ambulance and I knew..." Gary ran up to them then, panting, his face all red and puffy. Brian hugged him. It was all he could think to do.

"Tell his dad I've got him," Mark said, and Gary nodded. Brian, feeling as if he was in a dream, found himself focusing on something. Through his tears, in the distance, he saw his dad standing there on the street corner, watching. Why had he stopped?

Then Mark put Brian on his bike. Mark strapped his huge helmet on his head. It was heavy and smelt bad but it made the world disappear.

"Hold on to me really tight!" Mark shouted as he revved the engine.

And they sped off.

*

And suddenly the bike was stopping. Brian felt himself being pressed into Mark's back like when the bus stops and the people standing up fall forward. Mark switched off the engine, turned and lifted him down. It seemed to take him ages to undo the helmet's strap, and his fingers pinched Brian's skin a bit, but he didn't care. He got the helmet off Brian's head and just threw it to the floor.

They ran in to the hospital.

"Hello!" Mark shouted over the counter because there was no-one there. "Hey! Hello!"

A lady came in through a door behind the counter, and opened her mouth to speak. But Mark said, "My girlfriend, Emily Carpenter, is she here?"

"Oh yes, she arrived a few minutes ago." Mark slapped the counter and ran towards some double doors. Brian followed him.

"Em!" Mark was shouting. "Em!" A tall man in green overalls came through the doors. Mark yelled, "Out of my way!"

"Please sir, come and—"

"Out of my way! I want to see my girlfriend!"

"You must be Mark."

"Yes, I've got to—" Mark stopped suddenly. "Has she been asking for me then?"

"Yes. Now if you come and sit down I'll get you a coffee and we can talk about what happened."

"So she's conscious then?" Mark said.

"Yes, she was partially conscious when she arrived."

"Will she be okay?" Mark said slowly.

"Yes, she's going to be fine."

"Oh Jees, thank God. She's going to be fine!" Mark knelt down and gave Brian a big hug. Brian's eyes stung with tears, but these were tears of relief. Mark kissed his cheek, and stood up again.

"She's pregnant," he said to the doctor suddenly.

"I know." The doctor was leading them back towards all the chairs.

"So, will the baby be okay?"

"That is one of the things we are hoping to find out right now."

"Oh Jees," Mark said into his clenched fist.

Pregnant, Brian thought. Pregnant. She was going to have a baby? Who would its dad be? Perhaps *he* could be its dad! Perhaps Mark would be. Perhaps it could have two dads, Brian and Mark!

The doctor asked them to sit down. He patted Brian's shoulder, and said he would tell them as soon as there was any news about Emily. Mark sighed. He sat, and put his head in his hands. Brian wondered if he was crying, but couldn't tell. He looked at the picture on Mark's shoulder, the one of the dragon. He knew it was Mark's favourite because it had been there so long. All the others changed almost every week. Sometimes the jacket was covered in flowers and colour, sometimes in skeletons, sometimes just in strange shapes with writing coming out of them. But the dragon was always there, like a little pet, sitting on his shoulder.

Brian leant against Mark, and Mark put his arm around him. "She'll be okay, Mark," Brian said. "They'll both be okay."

Dad

Emily looked white. Her hair stuck out over the top of the giant bandage and made her look like a boy. Her eye makeup had run, and was smeared across her face. Most of the orange stuff she liked to put on her face had gone and underneath it she was as pale as Dragon, and her eyes were puffy.

She managed to smile though. Mark leaned over and hugged her. It seemed like ages before he let her go. Normally, Brian would have been making joke throwing-up noises, but not this time.

Then Mark sat down on a chair beside the bed, still holding Emily's hand.

Brian was standing. Emily smiled at him. He didn't know what to say, so just said, "Hello."

"Hello, Bri," said Emily, and ruffled his hair.

"Thought you were going to die," said Mark.

"Did you, Honey?" Emily smiled.

"Thought I was going to lose you."

"Well, I'm still here."

"Thought we'd lose our kid, too," Mark said.

Emily darted Mark a sharp glare.

"It's okay, Em," Mark said, "Bri knows."

"Really? You know, Bri?"

"About the baby?" Brian said. Emily nodded. "Mark told me."

"Well, aren't you going to congratulate us then, Bri?" smiled Emily.

"Yer," Mark said. "I'm gonna be a dad."

"Oh," Brian said, realising that he wouldn't be the dad after all.

"What do you think then, Bri?" asked Emily. "You'll be an uncle, he'll be your nephew!"

"Will I?"

"Yer, that'll be something to tell all your friends, won't it?"

"Yes, I'll tell Gary," Brian grinned. "He saved your life!"

"What?" Emily managed a weak frown of disbelief.

"Yer, his mum's a nurse. He moved you so you wouldn't choke. And he showed me how to stop your head bleeding. Will I really be an uncle?"

Emily smiled now and nodded. "And a wonderful one," she said, and Mark pulled Brian close to him, putting his arm round Brian's waist. Then, Emily and Mark talked for a little while about how Emily felt, what the nurses were like, and how long she'd have to stay in for. The doctor had said she'd been unconscious for a while and they wanted to keep her in, just in case. Brian wondered "just in case" what? But he didn't like to ask. She'd already had some special tests to check that she was okay, and she'd still have to have a few more. She would have to stay in for a day or two, but she would be home soon. She and the baby had been really lucky, the doctor had told her. And Brian suddenly had such a warm feeling inside. He would be an uncle! And Emily would come home with her baby and she and Mark and Brian and Dad would live together and look after it and everything would be alright forever! It reminded him of how he felt when he was with Dragon and Isabelle and the pigs: cosy, content, important and safe...

But then Mark's face changed. He looked sternly at Emily and said, "Now tell me straight, Em, did he hit you?"

"Who?"

"You know who. He did, didn't he? I'll kill him. I'll kill him."

"Do you mean Dad?" Emily said.

"You know I do."

"Well, no. I'm sure he wouldn't do that."

"What do you mean, you're *sure*? Can't you remember?"

"Well, I can remember the argument..."

"He did, didn't he?" hissed Mark. "Right," he announced, moving Brian and standing, "I'm going to sort him out."

"He didn't hit her," Brian said, but the lump in

his throat made it come out as a whisper.

"I'm going to sort him out, Em. No-one does that and gets away with it. He should be locked up."

"Mark," Emily held his hand again, "Mark, I don't think he—"

"Don't try and stop me Em, he can't get away with it."

"He didn't hit her," Brian managed again, a little louder this time.

"Okay, Babe, I won't hurt him, I'll just tell him he can't live there anymore. I'll tell him to go. Don't care where, I'll just tell him to get lost. He's dangerous. He's a drunk and he's gone too far."

"Mark!" Brian shouted. "Mark! He didn't hit her!"

"He can't get away with it Bri," Mark said. "I know he's your dad an' all, but..."

"But he didn't hit her, she slipped. I saw!"

Mark looked at him. "Are you sure?"

"I saw what happened. My dad didn't hit her. *She* hit *him*! And she slipped in some beer and fell." Brian forced his voice to be steady and clear, and he ignored the clouds in his eyes and the feeling of warm tears breaking down his cheeks. "She hit some chairs. That's what happened, I promise. Don't hurt Dad, please don't hurt him!"

Mark sat back down and pulled Brian towards him. He wiped Brian's face with his finger. Then he put his hands on Brian's arms. "Are you sure, Bri? I mean, you're not just covering up for him or something?"

"No! He wouldn't do that. He didn't hit her, she slipped, I saw! Gary saw too. Ask him if you don't believe me!"

"Mark," said Emily calmly, "he's right, I'm sure. He didn't hit me. He can be a bit... He can be a bit... But really, he wouldn't do that."

"Even so, if there was beer on the floor, that was his fault. It is his fault you're here, Em."

Suddenly, Brian saw his dad. He was standing there at the entrance to the ward, looking at Emily. She hadn't noticed him though. Brian wanted to smile at him, and wave, but didn't want Mark to see he was there.

"He didn't mean to spill the beer," Emily told Mark. "It was an accident. I can remember that."

"Em," said Mark, "you're always too nice about people, 'specially him. It was his fault. Of course it was. However it happened. And if I ever get the idea that he's hit you, or done something like that to you again, you know what I'll do. He won't get away with it."

Brian's dad was gazing at them, all alone, with nurses and patients pushing past him. Brian wanted to go and hug him, to take his strong hand and lead him over to Emily so everything could be alright again. But he couldn't, and after a few long moments, the big man lowered his head, turned and walked away.

Grown-ups Can't Be Friends
With Dragons

After Emily came home from hospital, Brian didn't go to see Dragon so often. He wanted to be close to Emily and Mark. He wanted to make sure Emily wasn't having any of the dizzy spells Gary had told him to watch out for. She didn't have the huge bandage round her head by the time she came home, but she did have a big padded plaster where the cut was. She was a bit shaky and weak, and Mark made her miss a few days of work and school. Brian did the washing up for her, and tidied his room without a fuss when she asked him to. He couldn't stop thinking about the baby. He was going to be an uncle! Emily had said she would want him to help the baby grow up to be kind and good and clever. Mark had told Brian he would have to "set the baby a good example," and help it to learn about the world. That meant he would have to stop getting into trouble. He was going to have to be like a grown-up.

Brian knew that grown-ups can't be friends with dragons. If he wanted to be a good uncle, he wouldn't be able to see Dragon and Isabelle so much anymore.

That made him painfully sad. Yet, whenever he was here in the real world, Dragon and Isabelle seemed so far away, like a dream. And sometimes, just sometimes, he even felt silly for ever having thought they were real.

He did go there sometimes, though. When he knew Emily didn't need him.

Today was the first time he had been for ages. Winter was behind them and the weather was getting a little warmer now, but still, he wore the thick coat his dad had given him for Christmas.

Things seemed different now, different in ways Brian couldn't understand. Dragon was pleased to see him, and asked where he'd been, and if he was okay. Brian said he was, but he knew Dragon could tell he wasn't. Brian had already told Dragon and Isabelle all about what had happened to Emily. He'd had to keep explaining what things were, like the telephone, and the ambulance. She said it all sounded like magic: a thing you could talk into to someone miles away, and a cart which drives without a horse! Dragon seemed to understand. He could see Brian's thoughts in a way that Isabelle couldn't. If Brian wanted to tell Dragon what something was like he just had to think about it.

They were both very excited when he told them about Emily's baby. He had expected Isabelle to say something like, "I didn't know ghosts could have babies," but she didn't. She understood a bit more about Brian and his world now.

But even after that, Brian knew something else was making him feel different. Something else was making him feel sad. Isabelle and Dragon noticed that too, but Brian didn't know why he was feeling that way.

"I'm sorry I haven't come here much recently," he said. "It's just... It's hard now. Things are changing. I might not be able to come so much now. I'll try, but..."

As he went back to his own world later that day, walking up the steep road from the harbour towards home, he stopped and looked behind him at the sea. It was a deep grey-green today. There were heavy clouds all across the sky, but in the distance the sun shone through onto the dark water, brightening it in golden stripes. There was a strong wind in the bay. The seagulls were being blown about like crisp packets in the playground.

Brian remembered the town he had visited with Isabelle; the strange pub, like this one, but so different. He knew now that Isabelle's world was here, but in the past.

He watched the sea, and realised it was exactly the same as in Isabelle's time. It never changed. Everything else had changed, but the sea hadn't.

Brian wished his life could be as simple as that.

Uncle Brian

Brian had wondered for a long time if Emily's belly would ever stop growing. It seemed she had been fat forever. And how grumpy she had been! All through the summer she'd been moaning about her feet hurting, her swollen ankles, her bad back.

Brian's dad had got some extra work, and his night shift was even longer. Brian only saw him when he was on his way out to work or on his way up to bed. Emily had said Dad was very tired because he was working so hard for them, earning money to buy food for everyone and to pay the bills. But Mark had told Brian that his dad had been spending all the money in the pub and there was hardly enough to live on. Mark had said he wanted to take Emily away from here. They would save up to get a flat somewhere. But Mark hadn't got a proper job, so they couldn't do that yet. Brian hoped and prayed they never would.

Sometimes Mark and Brian's dad would have to pass each other in the kitchen or on the stairs. They never said anything to each other. They never even looked at each other. Brian wished they would make friends. Dragon had said he still could not understand the people in Brian's world.

At school, Brian was not in Miss Neale's class anymore. Mr Morgan was his teacher now. He was an ugly looking man with black hair, a black moustache and was always in shorts or a tracksuit. Brian liked him though. He was funny, but Brian didn't always understand his jokes. Sometimes he only knew he was joking because Terry and Gary and some of the others were laughing.

One day Emily was rushed to hospital in an ambulance. Brian felt sick as he remembered when Emily had slipped and knocked herself out. But this visit to hospital was a happy one.

Brian wasn't allowed in the special room where Emily was. He had to sit outside and draw, until his dad arrived.

It seemed like forever before Mark came out of the room, wearing a funny green gown over his T-shirt and black trousers. He was grinning with delight. He told Brian and his dad the baby was a girl. Dad stood and put his hand out to Mark for a handshake. Brian watched, thinking, "Please shake his hand, Mark, please." And Mark did shake it. Brian smiled, and Dad said, "Congratulations, lad."

Soon, Emily and the baby were home together, and Mark was round all the time. He even spent the night sometimes, and Brian's dad knew about it and it was all okay.

Mark and Dad even talked to each other now too. Brian even saw them laughing together once. Dad actually seemed happy. He was working hard, and spending time looking after the baby. The baby seemed to have made everything better.

At first, Mark and Emily couldn't think of a name for the baby. Mark wanted Marilyn, because he liked an old film star from years and years ago who was called that, but Emily hated the idea.

Brian wanted to be near the baby all the time. He wanted to look at her, to touch her, to hold her on his lap. He wanted to smell her and to hear her tiny little baby-snore. He wanted to put his big finger in her tiny fist. He wanted to stroke her ears, and tickle her feet. Emily sometimes got cross with him and told him to leave the baby alone. He wanted them to hurry up and give her a name. He didn't like having to call her 'the baby' all the time.

At last, they settled on Laura. Brian didn't mind because everyone at school liked Laura Godley, so he felt that was a good name. Laura Godley didn't like him much, but that didn't matter anymore. He felt so grown up when he was looking after baby Laura.

When Brian's birthday arrived he didn't have many presents, but he understood because he knew that babies were expensive to look after, and Laura was better than any birthday present he could wish for. And he felt really happy.

He wasn't having much of a party, but he was having Gary and Terry round for tea. Emily was cooking dinner, then they'd have some videos, and the boys would sleep over.

At the end of school they all met in the playground. They kicked puddle-water at each other, and Brian got his old, holey trainers all soggy and his feet freezing cold.

The three boys walked home together.

"Will we see your sister's kid then?" asked Terry.

"You've seen her before," Brian said.

The rain had stopped, but everything seemed wet and grey and chilly.

Before long, they arrived at Brian's house. Emily was in the kitchen feeding Laura.

"Hello, Bri," she said. "Hi, Gary." She was always pleased to see Gary, especially after that terrible day. She always gave him biscuits and drinks of squash. "Hi, Terry."

"Alright?"

The three boys went upstairs. Terry complained that there was no TV in Brian's room. Brian felt ashamed and Gary looked as though he didn't know what to say.

Later, they had tea. Emily brought trays of food up to Brian's room, and smiled all the time. When she had gone, Terry whispered, "She's not bad after all," but Brian could see him smirking at Gary. Gary ignored him though. "What does she use on her hair?" Terry said. "Is it glue? It looks nice." Brian smiled, unsure whether Terry was being serious or making fun of Emily.

After tea, they went downstairs and watched a film. Mark had got it for them. They weren't old enough to watch it really, but he said it wouldn't hurt. Mark came in when the film was halfway through, and watched some with them. He'd obviously seen it hundreds of times because he sat on the edge of the sofa, and mouthed all the words, clenching his fists and shouting, "Yes! Get the sucker!" every now and then. But Emily called him from upstairs so he rolled his eyes and made them laugh by pretending to be Emily's humble, long-suffering servant, and off he went to help her with Laura.

A little later, Brian's dad came downstairs and made himself some toast. He stood in the doorway munching. Brian wondered what he was thinking. Was he watching the film or looking at him? "See ya, boys," he said, and went off to work. Brian waited for the comments from Terry, but there were none. Perhaps the film was too exciting.

They were allowed to stay up late after the film, but Emily came down eventually to send them off to bed. She didn't want the baby disturbed. She looked really tired; her eyes were red and her skin was pale. She looked funny with no makeup on. So different.

Soon the boys were all in Brian's room. Terry and Gary were in their sleeping bags on cushions on the floor, and none of them were sleepy. They laughed and joked. Sometimes they would suddenly realise how loud they were being and all fall silent at the same time, listening for footsteps on the landing. The first few times there were none, but eventually, Emily came into the room. She'd tiptoed so quietly that they hadn't heard her until the door opened.

"Can't you keep it down?" she said. "Laura's asleep and I don't want her waking up."

"Sorry, Mrs Carpenter," Terry said, as if he was the politest person in the world.

"It's *Miss* Carpenter," Emily corrected him.

"Sorry, Em," Gary said.

"It's alright, Gary," she said. "Try to go to sleep now boys, eh?" she added. They all assured her they would, so she said, "Good night," and quietly closed the door.

"She thinks she's your mum," said Terry. "Does she always boss you around? It's like being at school." Brian and Gary ignored the comment. "Hey," Terry whispered after a few moments of silence. "If I can't have Laura Godley, I'll have to have your baby sister, Bri, when she grows up!"

"She's not my sister, she's my niece."

"Hey Bri," Gary said, "I just remembered you're an uncle!"

"Uncle Brian!" Terry grinned. "Tell us a story Uncle Brian, oh please, Uncle Brian, please!" And they all started laughing again.

Burn the Witch! Kill the Pigs!

And then, one night, Brian heard Dragon's voice. At first it was in his dream, and he wondered why Dragon was there in school with him. The voice kept calling him, soft and gentle, yet urgent and serious, like when Emily wanted to wake him up. And he suddenly realised he was dreaming.

School vanished, and he felt himself warm and snug in his bed. But Dragon still called.

Brian jumped at first, shocked by hearing Dragon's voice here, away from the cave. He sat up and blinked in the pale orange glow of the nearby street lamp.

Dragon needed him. What could he do? He wanted to go back to sleep. He couldn't go to Dragon in the middle of the night, surely?

But Dragon's voice sounded worried, almost desperate. Brian couldn't hear words in the voice, he could just hear a sound like a cry. It wasn't one of pain, but of strong pleading. Brian knew he had to go to him.

He snuck quietly through the house, pulling on his coat as he stole down the stairs, careful not to use the creaky step. He found the key to the back door and soon was outside, in his wellingtons, in the cold, frightening night.

He squeezed the back door closed, and hurried down to the harbour. Soon he was fumbling his way across the dark, slippery rock. Moonlight had turned the beach pale silver and the shadows were thick and black. But it wasn't the darkness that frightened him. It was the worry in Dragon's voice.

"We must go to Isabelle," Dragon said when Brian at last clambered through the cave and made his way towards his friend. "She has been calling. She is in trouble, I know it. This is the day when I must help her!"

Brian's heart was pounding as he climbed into the space beside Dragon and soon the images began to form. Slowly they became objects, and he saw moonlight, and trees. He could smell smoke, and see specks of orange light in the distance, moving away through the forest. He could hear the voices of men shouting in the darkness.

"Something terrible is happening," said Dragon, and suddenly he began to rush through the forest towards Isabelle's house. Brian, chilled both by fear and by the cold night air, followed.

As they came closer to the clearing, the smoke seemed to get thicker and thicker, illuminated from within by a bright orange blur, and he could feel a strange warmth. The air was filled with a vicious crackling sound, and as they approached the clearing, they realised that was where it came from. "Isabelle!" called Dragon, horror in his voice now. Where the house had been, a huge mountain of fire engulfed Isabelle's hollow tree. Brian could feel the smoke passing through him, warming him and choking him at the same time. Millions of tiny sparks swirled around him like fiery snow.

He heard a creak. He looked up and saw a huge, old, burning branch sag. Then it fell. It dropped through the smoke making it curl and recoil. It crashed into the fire and a volcano of sparks erupted.

Brian quickly searched around for signs of Isabelle and the pigs, but he was suddenly aware that Dragon was speeding towards the fire.

"Dragon!" he yelled. "Dragon! Come back!" He raced after him, feeling the heat burning through him.

"She must be in here!" called Dragon. "I must find her!" Brian followed him, feeling every spark and piece of smouldering wood that fell through him. Flames tore at him as he forced himself to stay close to Dragon. Somehow, being parted from his friend felt worse than following him into the fire.

Now there was only fire. All around him and in him. He could see nothing. He knew Dragon was there somewhere, but he could not find Isabelle, not even a feeling of her.

At last Dragon was beside him again. "She's not here," he said. Thankfully, Brian pulled himself out and the cool air washed the heat away.

Dragon was heading away from the clearing now, along a forest path. Brian followed.

"Where are we going?" he cried.

"To find Isabelle!"

"Where will she be?"

"I don't know, but I can feel her calling now. She is close to us."

In the distance ahead of them they could see orange lights among the trees, and hear the sound of men's voices.

Suddenly, Dragon left the path and sped into the dark forest, whizzing over brambles and bracken. Brian followed. Some of the trees looked silver in the moonlight.

"Isabelle!" said Dragon, and he suddenly heard delighted gasps.

"Dragon? Brian? Is that really...?"

They found Isabelle curled up in a shallow hollow. There was bracken and trees all round her. She was shivering with cold and fear. She was holding Mary and Beelzebub to her sides, but Brian couldn't see Jesus. Isabelle's eyes were red and her cheeks were wet and dirty.

"Isabelle," Brian said.

"My dear, dear friends," she sobbed, in a hoarse whisper.

"What's happening?" Dragon asked.

"Oh my... oh Lord, I can hardly bring myself to tell you." She sobbed loudly and wiped her nose with the back of her hand. Mary and Beelzebub snorted and sniffed at Brian and Dragon. He could tell they were scared too. They seemed to understand something bad was happening, and they didn't want to leave Isabelle's side. "They wants to kill me," Isabelle said. "And I can't find Jesus! He ran off into the woods, all scared. Oh please don't let them get him. They'll kill him! They're evil men."

"Don't worry," Brian said, moving towards her. "We'll find him. He'll be alright."

Around them they could hear the voices. Angry voices. Shouting. They sounded closer now. The smell of smoke was really strong.

"We can't stay here," said Dragon. "They're coming this way."

"Oh Lord," said Isabelle. "They'll kill me. They thinks I'm a witch. That fella down at the harbour, the one Mary bit, he got ill. They all blame me; they think it's my witchcraft, but it isn't. I don't know any witchcraft. Hunters found out where I live. They burned down my house!"

"Come on," said Dragon, "this way." Isabelle followed Dragon's voice out of the hollow and through the undergrowth which tore her clothes. She stooped low, and told the two pigs to go in front of her. They trotted along, snorting. Their ears were back, flat to their heads. Their sides were scratched from the brambles.

The voices were behind them now.

Isabelle muttered words to herself which sounded like magic spells. Brian couldn't tell what she was saying, but occasionally he would catch the word, "Jesus."

"We'll find him," he whispered.

Because Brian and Dragon couldn't be seen, they were able to go up above the undergrowth and see which direction looked safest. That way, they led Isabelle through the forest. The men's voices stayed in their ears, a short distance behind them, never going away. Isabelle dared to look over her shoulder, and gasped at the sight of the orange lights which Brian now realised must be burning torches.

And suddenly, as they came to a ridge from where the ground sloped steeply downwards, they saw men in front of them too, coming up the slope. The torches appeared as though from nowhere and the voices were close. Dragon stopped. Isabelle dropped to the floor, brambles scratching her face. She grabbed the two pigs and held them round their necks, commanding them to be quiet. They obeyed.

"What can we do now?" she gasped. Dragon said nothing. "Oh poor old Jesus, he must be in a right panic, I've got to find him; he'll think I've deserted him!"

The torches and the voices got even nearer. Then it seemed that Dragon had gone again. At that moment, Mary pulled away from Isabelle, and ran straight at the men. Isabelle reached out for Mary hissing a desperate command. But Mary paid no attention. She disappeared into the shadows.

There were some shouts from the men. Suddenly they were yelling, "Over 'ere!" and, "It's one of 'er pigs!" and, "Grab it!" The torches began to move away from Isabelle, Beelzebub and Brian, and they knew that Mary was being chased.

Mary *and Dragon*, Brian realised!

Isabelle was sobbing now. "Mary, oh my dear Mary, please come back, oh Mary, come back, please!"

"Dragon is with her," Brian said. "He's leading her! Look, we can escape now." Brian led Isabelle forwards until they came to the path where the men had been standing. All was quiet and deserted now. The forest was dark around them.

Not knowing where he was going, Brian led Isabelle and Beelzebub along the path, away from the voices. They moved as fast as they could, which was only as fast as Beelzebub's slow trot.

"Where can we go?" Isabelle gasped. Brian didn't reply, because he didn't know. They kept moving. Brian knew Isabelle and Beelzebub were running for their lives, and he was their only hope.

Then, as they rounded a bend, Brian's heart flipped. "Stop! Stop!" he hissed at Isabelle. Four men were coming slowly towards them. Isabelle skidded to a stop, and put her hand down to stop Beelzebub. The men were stooping low, and weren't holding torches. Brian realised they were sneaking along in the darkness, hoping they'd run into Isabelle, and they had. "Run!" he yelled at Isabelle, but he could see the men had already spotted her. They ran at her and Beelzebub. Isabelle turned, but she wasn't fast enough. Shouting cruelly, the men grabbed her by the arms and surrounded her. They didn't pay much attention to Beelzebub, and he trotted back down the path a short way. He turned round and came back towards them, frightened and confused.

Brian felt so stupid. He'd let them down so badly. He was supposed to be helping them but he'd led them directly into trouble. "I'm sorry, Isabelle!" he called. "I'm sorry!" and he swore at himself several times. He didn't even know if Isabelle had heard him. She was doing some swearing of her own, as the men pulled her around and yelled at her to stop struggling.

Further down the track, where the men had come from, something large moved in the darkness. It was only the occasional blotches of moonlight that enabled Brian to see it was a cart being pulled along by two big horses. Another man was leading them on foot. He wasn't holding a torch either.

The men dragged Isabelle towards the cart. The man leading the horses made them stop now.

Two of the men came storming towards Beelzebub, waving big sticks. "Get lost, pig!" they growled, and charged threateningly at him. The poor pig started, ears back, but did not run away. "I said get lost, pig!" growled one man. Still Beelzebub did not run, but he shrank back in fear.

Brian whispered to Beelzebub, "It's okay, it's okay." But he knew it wasn't.

The man reached inside his fur tunic and pulled something out. At first, Brian couldn't see what it was, but, as the man pointed it right at Beelzebub, the moon light glinted blue on the metal tube...

Isabelle was screaming, "Run, Beelzebub, run! He's going to kill you!" Brian's heart froze.

The man began to laugh. Others around him urged him on.

Brian dropped down to Beelzebub's ear and tried to get the pig to follow him, but he wouldn't.

"Go on, Thomas, shoot it!" The man, Thomas, was pointing the pistol right at Beelzebub. Isabelle screamed and screamed but Beelzebub did not turn and run. He stood in the path, refusing to leave Isabelle.

But then Brian had another idea. He moved quickly over to the two horses which were pulling the cart. The pigs could hear him, so maybe the horses could too. He went between them and forced out a scream as terrifying and loud as he could possibly manage.

The horses reared up. They kicked their hooves in the air and snorted like lorry engines.

The gun went off with a surprisingly soft pop, but even so, Brian heard the bullet zip through the air.

Birds in the trees went flying off into the night. Beelzebub made a horrible noise. Fear or pain? Brian didn't have time to see before the pig lumbered off into the undergrowth.

The men were suddenly all trying to control the horses and they let go of Isabelle. She dropped to her knees as the grip on her arms was released.

Brian let out another scream, even more powerful than his first one. He drove the noise right into the ear of one of the horses, and then into the ear of the other. The creatures reared again. One of the men got a hoof in the face and blood covered his cheek instantly. He gripped his head and staggered back, shouting.

The horses panicked. They broke into a run, the

cart bouncing along behind them as they vanished into the blackness. Some of the men chased it round the bend in the path and out of sight. The others gathered around Isabelle.

"What did you do to the horses, witch?" shrieked the man with the bloody face. He came over. The whole side of his head was covered in blood now which, in the cold moonlight, looked like black paint. Isabelle didn't reply. Brian could see her looking past the men towards where Beelzebub had gone. One of the men grabbed her arm and pulled her to her feet. Another shouted into the woods, "We've got her, boys!"

Brian felt himself filling with an intense sickness of sorrow and guilt. He heard Isabelle's sobs, and wondered if she knew he was still there.

There was the sound of horses' hooves, and round the bend came the horses he had scared away. Three exhausted, red faced men led them.

"I told the others," one of the men said. "They're on their way over here now."

"Good," said the man who was holding Isabelle. "Help me get her in the cart." Quickly, they tied Isabelle's hands behind her back, and lifted her onto the wooden slats. She didn't put up a fight.

"What about the pig?" said another.

"Ah, it ran off. Think I got it though."

"We'll find it in the morning then," said the first

man. "It'll make a grand feast for us what's earned it." At that, Isabelle struggled, kicking her legs and twisting her body. One of the big men thumped her across the face. She became still, but gave him such an evil glare. Then she spat blood right at him. He wiped it off his face, and hit her again. Brian raced at the man and screamed at him, but just passed right through him without the man even noticing. Blood and saliva hung from Isabelle's chin now.

The huge horses, still acting a bit nervous, began to pull the cart slowly along the muddy path.

There was a bright moon behind the trees.

"Dragon..." Isabelle muttered. "Brian, save us... spirits, save us."

"What's she sayin'?" asked one of the men.

"Dunno," said another, but if she don't shut up I'll belt her again." Brian was burning with fury, the same way he felt when Terry was winding him up. But this was much worse, and he knew he was helpless. He wondered where Dragon had gone. He wanted to leave the cart and search in the woods for him and Mary. He wanted to find Jesus, too, who could be anywhere. But he knew he couldn't leave Isabelle.

Beelzebub was still close by though. He could hear the undergrowth rustling and he even caught a glimpse of the pig's spiny pink back.

"It's alright Isabelle," he said. "Dragon will be

back soon to help us. We'll save you."

Isabelle nodded.

"Hey!" came a shout from the front of the cart. "What the devil...?" At the same time, there was a sound like applause, and Brian looked round. The air above the trees seemed to be moving. It was a blizzard of black shapes which seemed to be constantly changing, flickering and flashing silver in the moonlight. A cacophony of screaming and squawking terrified him for a moment, and then he realised what he was seeing. A flock of huge black ravens was swooping down from the trees, their dark wings clapping together excitedly.

It happened so fast: the ravens thundered low over the cart and the driver jumped to the ground, his hands over his face in defence. Another man cried out and dived from the cart. As the birds went overhead, Brian felt the wind from their wings. It wasn't just ravens now, but there were pigeons and owls and other kinds of birds too. Their feathers drifted about calmly amongst the mayhem.

"Blimey," shouted the man who had hit Isabelle. "What kind of magic...?" But another wave of birds came diving towards him, screeching and grabbing at the men with their sharp claws. The air was full of birds now. The noise was deafening. The men shouted and waved their arms about and dropped off the cart to the ground. The birds were tearing out their hair and gouging their skin with their sharp claws and beaks. Brian suddenly noticed they were leaving Isabelle alone though. She was smiling up at them all, her hair fanned by their wings, feathers settling on her head and shoulders like snow. A couple of the men rolled under the cart for safety. The horses had stopped and were snorting, and stamping their feet, but not rearing up.

Only one man was left on the cart now. He was the one who had shot at Beelzebub. He lay flat against the floor, and the birds kept on attacking him.

"Call them off, witch!" he shouted.

"Never!" hissed Isabelle, as more birds swooped down. "Not until you get off the cart!" and she kicked him in the chest with both feet. The man curled himself up, hugging his bleeding head in his arms, and coughing as Isabelle kicked the air out of his lungs. Brian thought she was going to break his ribs. She was tougher than any old woman he'd ever met.

Still the birds attacked. There were all kinds of different types, and even the tiniest birds attacked fiercely. Feathers swirled around in the air. The man wriggled his way to the back of the cart, and dropped off it. He fell to the muddy ground with a thump. The birds tore at him as he scrambled to his feet and ran. The two from under the cart joined him and they made their desperate escape, stumbling and bumping into each other as the birds attacked.

Brian realised that, even though there had been all the screeching and shouting, the horses had stayed calm.

And suddenly he saw the dark shapes of two pigs, trotting up to the cart. Isabelle sat up, fighting with the ropes around her hands.

"Oh, Dragon, you found them!"

"We must hurry now." Brian was pleased to hear Dragon's voice and to feel him near. Behind them he saw the orange lights, and heard the angry shouts.

"What about Beelzebub?" Isabelle whispered.

"Don't worry," Brian said. He quickly went to where he had last seen the frightened and injured pig. He looked around for a moment, and found him hiding nearby. Beelzebub came towards Brian's voice, limping. Brian spoke reassuringly to him and quickly tried to see where he was hurt. Beelzebub sniffed the air where Brian was. It was too dark among the bracken to see the pig's wound, but he was still on his feet, so Brian led him back through the undergrowth.

They came out of the bushes onto the path.

"Beelzebub!" Isabelle cried. Mary and Jesus nudged Beelzebub with their noses. It was as if they were saying, "Hello."

Then Isabelle gasped. A large owl had landed on the cart and started pulling at her ropes.

"Dragon, you're a miracle worker!" she grinned. "Come up, pigs!" she cried while the owl nipped and tore, and Brian found himself fascinated by its huge, bright, glassy eyes. "You'll have to jump up," Isabelle called. Mary seemed to understand. She leapt, catching her trotters on the wood. For a moment she hung there, her back legs dangling in the air, but then she fell to the mud. She rolled over and scrambled to her feet.

Isabelle's hands were free. The owl flew off beating the air with its wings. Isabelle threw the ropes away and jumped down from the cart.

She grabbed Mary round the belly, and, with an enormous effort, lifted her to the cart. Mary scrabbled at the wood and pulled herself aboard.

The shouting was close now; Brian could even hear the words.

"She's 'ere! I can see the cart! Come on!"

"Look out, she'll 'ave some tricks left yet!"

"This time just shoot 'er!"

Isabelle went up to Beelzebub. Brian could see the pig was shaking. There was a wound on his leg which he hadn't been able to see before, and a dark trickle of blood ran from it. Isabelle stroked him, and said something in his ear. Then she put her arms around his fat belly and lifted him. He whimpered and flinched.

"Come on, Beelzebub," Brian said.

"Come on, my friend," Dragon tried.

Isabelle heaved at him. He gave a little jump too, but Isabelle staggered back and they both fell into the mud.

"This way!" shouted a voice. Brian could smell the smoke of the burning torches again. At least the incident with the birds had left the men scared and cautious; they were hanging back, for now. But one of them had a pistol, he remembered. Maybe they could kill Isabelle without even needing to come any closer.

Isabelle got to her feet and tried again to lift Beelzebub into the cart. Brian desperately wanted to help, but couldn't do much. All he and Dragon could do now was try to encourage Beelzebub, and hope he understood. Mary was standing on the cart, looking at Isabelle and Beelzebub. Isabelle tried again. This time, Beelzebub's front legs were on the cart. Mary nosed at Beelzebub's face. Then she put her mouth around his ear. She was trying to pull him on! And Jesus came up behind him and pushed his head against Beelzebub's backside. Beelzebub's hind legs were kicking about. He probably didn't know he was kicking Jesus's face, and Jesus put up with it and kept on pushing his brother. Isabelle made a loud groan of effort, and Beelzebub was suddenly safely aboard.

The men were very close now. They were so close Brian could see their faces lit up by the fire of the torches.

"Shoot 'er!" someone commanded.

"What happens if you kill a witch though?" came the fearful reply. "I don't want my family cursed."

Isabelle grabbed hold of Jesus. She gave a really loud shout, and, as he jumped, she practically threw him on board. She was so strong, Brian didn't even think of her as 'old' anymore.

Then, Isabelle threw herself onto the cart.

"The horses, Brian," Dragon said.

Brian quickly went to the front of the cart. He didn't want to scare the horses anymore, but he did want to get them moving. He called softly to them, "Go, horses!" and they galloped off as if they had completely understood everything that was happening.

The cart lurched about all over the place as its wooden wheels hit rocks and roots. It slid around in the muddy ruts that the wheels of other carts had made. Brian left the horses and went back into the cart. Isabelle gripped the wooden sides, and pulled Jesus to her. Mary fell onto her knees as the cart bounced, and then gave up trying to stand. She lay down next to Beelzebub.

Beelzebub was lying down too. Isabelle stroked

his head.

Soon they were out of the forest and onto the cliff path. Beneath them, the sea was black.

They raced on.

"We'll have to slow down!" yelled Isabelle. "We'll smash the wheels! Slow the horses down Brian!"

He didn't really know how. It was easy to make them run, but he didn't know how to make them slow down. He said some soothing words to them and made some gentle sounds. Again, seeming to understand, they slowed down and walked. They had left the men far behind them now, and they couldn't even see the fires or smell the smoke anymore.

"My poor Beelzebub," Isabelle said. "My poor, loyal friend." She looked at the wound. She ran her fingers round it and wiped some of the blood away with her skirt. She smiled. "It's just a scrape, yer big baby!" she said, and slapped his rump. As if in response, Beelzebub got to his feet and grunted at her. "No, lay down," she told him, and he did. Then, with the other pigs nosing at her and Beelzebub, she took a little pouch from her belt and began crushing leaves with her fingers, chewing them, and spitting them back into her palm. Then, she pressed the substance onto Beelzebub's wound. All the while, the pig sat there, unflinching. At last, Isabelle tore a strip from her skirt and tied it round Beelzebub's leg.

"Will he be alright?" Brian asked.

"He'll be fine. Was it you, Brian, who made them horses rear up? You saved him, you did. That man was aiming right between his eyes!"

"It was easy," Brian said, proud that he had done something useful. But then he remembered how he'd failed to spot the men in the first place. "I led you right to them though," he said apologetically. "It was my fault."

"Rubbish! You led us far away from the main group, remember. We was unlucky to get caught by them fellas, but they was only a small group. It'd have been much worse if it was all them others who caught us. Besides, you found us a cart! Thank you," Isabelle smiled. "Thank you both. You saved us."

They trundled gently on, the dark forest on one side and the black ocean on the other.

"Isabelle," Brian said after a while. "Why did they want to kill you?"

"They're dim, and stupid. They thought I cursed them. Remember that fella who kicked Mary the other day when we went into town? Well he got sick. Very sick. Can't eat. Anything he does eat turns to water and comes straight out the other end. Or comes back up again. He's wasting away, apparently. They thinks I cursed 'im. Idiots. My medicines makes people better, not sick. If they'd come to me as a friend, I might have been able to help him."

It was a cold night, but Isabelle looked comfortable and warm between her pigs.

"What will you do now?" Dragon asked.

"Well, I can't go back there. I don't know. What would you do?"

"I'd... just keep going," Dragon said. "Find another place. Find some people to help, with your medicines and potions."

"Yes," Brian agreed. "Don't come back here. It's not safe here." But, even as he said it, he found himself wondering what that would mean. Would he and Dragon still be able to visit Isabelle if she lived far away?

"Isabelle," Dragon said. "Do you remember that blue stone you showed us?"

"I certainly do," Isabelle said.

"Have you still got it?"

"I always keeps one with me, in my pouch."

"Can I see it again?"

Quickly, Isabelle produced the stone and held it up for Dragon and Brian. It seemed to be glowing this time, casting a pale blue light against Isabelle's face. As Brian gazed even closer, he realised that the dark veins within the stone didn't just form the random squiggles nature creates, but something more structured, neater, more repetitive. They were like the patterns on the tunnel walls which led to Dragon's dark cavern.

"There were more in my house," Isabelle added sadly. "I wonder if they'll have survived the fire."

"What are they, Dragon?" Brian asked. "Are they magic?"

"I think... they are ancient. Older than the Earth. Important somehow, but I'm still not sure what they are."

Isabelle sat back against the wall of the cart, admiring the stone for a moment. Then she tucked it away in her pouch and smiled.

"I'll keep it safe," she said, "and when you've remembered what it is, you'd best come and tell me."

"I don't think that will be possible," said Dragon sorrowfully. "We will have to leave you soon, Isabelle." Somehow, Brian had expected that.

Isabelle said, "But you will come back, won't you?"

"I don't think we can anymore," said Dragon.

"Why not?" Brian pleaded.

"Well," Dragon said, "I will try to explain. I have remembered some of where I am from, and why I am here. I came from a long way away; a different world."

"You mean, space?" Brian said.

"I believe so."

"You've lost me, you two," Isabelle said. "What's space?"

"Where the stars are," Brian said, "um... Yes."

"You're from the stars are you? Like angels?"

"I'm not," Brian said. "Only Dragon."

"Oh, of course," Isabelle said, "I still keeps forgetting you're a little boy who goes to school."

But Dragon ignored them both. He knew time was running out.

"There were lots of us. We were life-makers. We would bring life to new worlds, and help it survive and change. We moved through time like you move through space," Dragon went on. "We were travelling the universe at the end of time, and at the beginning. This planet had no life, so we made life here. Then we stayed, up above the planet, and watched it grow and change, and we helped it."

Isabelle just listened, amazed.

"Something went wrong, though. Our..." Dragon used one of his strange, musical words which Brian couldn't understand, and the picture Dragon showed him in his mind didn't help much either: it was a vast, dark, mountain-sized machine speckled with tiny lights and dotted with lumps and nodules, and there were dark holes like gaping mouths and long, trailing tentacles like the whiskers of a catfish, and it moved between the stars, around suns, from planet to planet... Brian certainly didn't know what it was. So Dragon said, "Our *cart*... fell out of the sky."

"Your cart?" Isabelle said.

"It wasn't a cart like this one. It was much, much bigger. And beautiful. And it went... *everywhere*."

"Did you hear that, Pigs? The angels travel in carts!" Isabelle's eyes were wide with awe.

"It was a spaceship!" Brian suddenly realised, his curiosity getting the better of his sadness for a moment.

"Yes, that's a good word for it," Dragon agreed. "And it fell to Earth."

"The spaceship crashed," Brian said, thinking aloud. "So, where are all the other dragons?" he asked.

"They must be dead, otherwise I would see their minds. My cavern would be lit up with them, like stars and suns. I'm the only survivor. Now I am powerless to help the life we created. But I *can* help *individuals*, if they know how to call for help in the right way. Once, when all life was young, there were voices around me all the time. Not people, like you, but beings, creatures, animals. When life was new on this planet, I could hear it all, and it could hear me, but as the planet grew older, and life changed, the world grew darker, until I was alone in my cave. I didn't even know whether there was still any life left. And The Magic put me into a deep, dark sleep, almost like death, and it kept me that way, so I would live longer, until rescue came, but it never did."

"What *magic*?" Isabelle asked, almost breathless with the effort of following Dragon's tangled tale.

"The Magic is a living force which used to guide me and the others like me. We were all part of it. The Magic connected us with those who needed help. And it still guides me, though the ability to hear me and to connect with me has faded from this world. But you did hear me, both of you. The Magic connected all three of us so that Brian and I could come through time to find you, Isabelle, and help you."

"I didn't hardly understand a single word of all that," Isabelle said, grinning sadly, "But you are my guardian angels." She wiped a tear from her cheek with a muddy hand. "I thought you would both be with me forever. I wish I didn't have to leave this place. I will miss you both so much. We all will." She hugged the pigs. "Maybe we'll be able to come back one day. Maybe you can visit me here again."

"The Magic connected us so we could help you," Dragon explained, "and we have done that." There was a deep melancholy in his voice now. "Our time with you... is over."

"Isabelle..." Brian began, but he could already feel Isabelle's world fading. He cried out to her.

Even though she couldn't see Brian, Isabelle smiled straight at him, and reached out her hand as if she was stroking his face.

A huge sadness choked him. This time, it seemed so... final. He tried desperately to hold on to the reality of the forest. He tried to make it stay. He looked into Isabelle's eyes.

"We'll always be here, in the forest," she whispered.

And then the darkness of the cave was all around them again.

"Don't be sad, Brian," said Dragon. "We have helped Isabelle. We have saved her. Be happy."

It was a long, long time before Brian spoke. "What would have happened if we hadn't been there?" he asked at last, swallowing the lump in his throat.

"Do you remember me once telling you that Isabelle came down here, to the cave, long ago, when I was in my sleep?" Dragon said.

"Yes."

"Well, that was what happened after the men came. They hunted her. She barely escaped with her life and she hid in the cave. She didn't have the pigs with her..."

"They k... They killed the pigs?"

"Yes. I think so. And... They caught Isabelle too, in the cave. She hadn't seen the tunnel which you found. Remember, I was sleeping then, and alone. I couldn't go to her like I can when you are here with me. I could hear her, in my dream, and she could hear me, but I couldn't go to her because, if I am to travel away from here, to other places and times, to help people, I need to connect with another mind first, like we do, you and I. But I was alone. And, that night, everything happened so quickly. Before I could properly talk to her, the men found her. I felt her fear. I felt her pain. And then... she wasn't there anymore. But we have saved her from that now."

"You mean... That won't happen now?"

"That's right. We went back to Isabelle's time and changed it. We have saved her."

Brian let out a long breath of relief.

"But... We'll never see her again," Brian said after a long silence.

"Isabelle lived a long, long time ago, for you at least. Hundreds of years ago. That's a tiny speck of time for me, but for you that is many lifetimes ago."

"She said they would always be there, in the forest," Brian said.

"Yes," Dragon said in a thoughtful voice.

"Does she mean... like ghosts?" Brian asked.

"Sort of."

"I don't understand. We were a bit like ghosts. You and me. Weren't we?"

"We were. And I think you will understand what

Isabelle meant," Dragon said. "One day."

A Dragon Lives Forever...

Laura was sitting on her mat, propped up by cushions, pulling some of her new toys out of her toy box and dispersing them around her. It was a few days after her first birthday, and every surface in the front room seemed covered in colourful cards.

"Laura," Emily moaned. "Look at all the mess." She ran her fingers through her hair. Her face was quite red. "Put some of that stuff back in the box please, darling." Brian could see she was gritting her teeth. Laura just looked at her and smiled.

"Come on Gaz," Brian said, let's go.

"Oh cheers, Brian!" Emily shouted, waving a tea towel at him, "leave me with all this will you!"

Brian kissed Laura and she held her arms up for him to hug her. He picked her up and squeezed her, making her giggle. He told Emily he'd help her later, even though he knew she'd probably have done all the washing up by then. But there were always plenty of other things to do. He and Gary went outside.

The evening air was cool, and it was getting dark already. The street lamps had just come on and it looked as if it might rain.

"Terry said he'd meet us up on the field," said Gary.

They pulled their jackets tight round them, and looked up at the clouds. They walked along the main road through town. Up here, it was a different world from the tiny, quiet harbour down below. The main road was lined with chip shops and hotels, and there was even a nightclub. You could see the sea from up here when you walked past the crazy golf course or the rock garden, but it seemed a long way away. Tonight, the sea was dark, cold and choppy.

They crossed over the road and climbed the hill away from the sea, towards the playing field. They called it a playing field anyway, but really it was just a big park with lumpy grass, not much good for football with all its potholes and bumps and the fairly steep slope. At the top of the field there were some swings, a roundabout, and a rusty old climbing frame. They often met there these days. They would talk, sometimes about girls, especially if Terry was there, or swap football stickers, or chase each other round the place.

Terry was waiting for them tonight. As Brian and Gary approached, Terry picked up a stick that was so thick and heavy it was almost a log, and threw it high into the air above them. Brian and Gary looked up at it, watched it spinning, and dived out of the way. The stick landed in the wet grass with a thud.

Brian swore at Terry, and ran to grab it. Suddenly it was a race, the three of them charging at it. They leapt at it, and rolled over, fighting and laughing. Gary got the stick, and escaped from the bundle. He charged down the slope a short way, then just hurled it up high, over his head towards Brian and Terry. Brian watched it falling, but couldn't seem to make a decision which way to go, and just curled up on the grass.

The stick came down across his back.

"Ow!" he yelled, and swore. Terry was laughing.

"Oh my God!" said Gary. "Sorry Bri! You okay?" Brian rolled over and didn't move. "Brian?" Gary came closer, stood over him.

Brian, uninjured and grinning secretly, grabbed Gary's legs and pulled him over, and a friendly scrap ensued.

At last, with their clothes all wet and muddy, they went over to the children's roundabout. They sat on it facing outwards, and turned it slowly with their feet.

"D'you want to hear the latest on my love-life then?" said Terry.

"Go on then," Gary said.

"Only Laura Godley. Fancied her for ages!"

"Oh," Brian said, trying to sound pleased.

"D'you remember when you kicked the ball and it hit her leg?" said Terry with a grin. "I thought she was going to kill you." Terry always remembered embarrassing things that happened years ago.

"Shut up."

"Ain't she beautiful when she's angry?"

"Shut up," Brian said, and forced a grin.

"It was funny though," Terry went on. "I nearly wet myself! I thought she'd turned into a teacher."

Gary smiled. "She scared my pants off!" he said.

"Yer," Terry continued, "scared nearly all Brian's clothes off. It's like he was running through the playground with no clothes on! It was funny. Eh Bri? It was a good one!"

Brian pretended to laugh.

"When did you start going out with her then, Tezza?" Gary said.

"The other day. She asked me. She said, 'Hey, dude, hows about you and I get it together?'"

"She never said that," Brian said.

"She did," Terry insisted. "She said, 'Hey muscle man!'" He pretended to flex his muscles. They laughed. "She said, 'Lover boy, I'm yours!'"

Terry prattled on for ages about him and Laura. Then they sat on the swings and Terry lobbed little stones at them, making them flinch and grin.

After a while, they wandered off across the field, stopping when they found a stone or a stick, and hurling it casually at mysterious objects in the twilight.

The three boys came to the edge of the field, far away from the swings and the telephone box and the houses. There was a high fence here made of wire. The trees of the forest poked their leaves and twigs through its diamond shaped holes.

"Let's climb over," said Terry.

"It's too high," Gary said.

"Step aside," Terry said dramatically. He marched towards the fence with his fists clenched like some kind of warrior. He gripped the wire mesh and began to climb. With the help of a tree branch and the metal fence post, he pulled himself over and dropped down into the shadows on the other side. He waved his arms victoriously, and soon all three of them were over and in the woods.

There was a soggy piece of carpet there, surrounded by cigarette ends and beer cans. Following Terry, they walked away from the fence and into the forest's gloom.

Brian had the strong sense of having been here before, though he was pretty sure he hadn't. The only time he'd really been into a forest was on a school trip once, and that had been a bus ride away. He'd been in the forest with Dragon and Isabelle of course, but those memories were distant and vague now, and he sometimes even wondered if they'd ever happened at all. The real world just made all that seem so... impossible.

The trees dripped cold water onto them. Terry picked up a soggy stick and threw it into the trees. A shower of rain water came down from the leaves and branches and the stick crashed away somewhere in the darkness.

They carried on walking, even though it was hard to see now. All the time, Brian felt that the place was familiar.

Brian's visits to the cave had become less and less frequent over the years. He loved going there, but it was hard to get away now that Emily needed so much help with Laura. Somehow, his old friend, Dragon, had begun to slip from his mind, and from his life too.

"Brian?" Gary called. "You okay? Come on!" He and Terry were already some way off down the path, two colourless, twilit silhouettes. Brian blinked, and headed off after them.

They walked for a long time, Gary and Terry talking and messing around, and Brian saying very little. The forest closed around them, and Brian felt himself disappearing into its shadows.

When did he last visit Dragon? He could barely remember, and he suddenly felt sick with guilt at having left his friend alone for so long. More than anything, Brian suddenly wanted to be there with him, sharing memories in the cavern's cold blackness.

"Dragon." He hadn't meant to say it aloud, he just, sort of, blurted it out without realising.

"What?" Gary said.

"Oh... Nothing."

"Did you say 'Dragon'?" Terry interrupted.

"No."

"You did. I heard you. You said 'Dragon'. Not that imaginary friend you used to have! Don't tell me you... D'you think he's here?" Terry began looking around. "Dragon!" he called. "Dragon! Where are you?"

"Shut up," Brian snapped.

"Yes," Gary agreed. "Leave it, Tez."

But Brian turned away. He didn't want to be here anymore. He wanted to go to Dragon, yet Dragon seemed so far away these days.

"I'm going back."

"What, scared of the dark or something?" Terry said.

"You alright, Bri?" Gary asked.

"I just... I don't feel well. A bit sick," he said, which wasn't a lie. "I should have stayed and helped Emily too."

And, ignoring Terry's mocking comments, he turned back the way they'd come. But he didn't want to go back. Somehow, just being here had stirred something within him. He remembered the first time he met Dragon, and their earliest visits to the forest, before Isabelle could even see or hear them. Sparks of electric joy danced in his belly at the memory, but they also felt swamped by a darker feeling, a sadness he couldn't understand. He was afraid he might cry. He walked away from the others, his eyes misting over with memories and moisture, but he didn't head for home.

"Where you going Bri?" Gary called as Brian headed deeper into the forest. "It's getting dark. Come on."

"Oh my god," Terry laughed. "You're scared of the dark, Gaz!"

"I am not," Gary objected. "Shut up Terry."

Brian was dimly aware that his friends were following him as he picked his way through bracken and brambles. The place seemed so familiar, as if it was the same trees growing here as in Isabelle's time, and they were welcoming him back.

Nettles and brambles billowed around his legs, but Brian kept going. Gary and Terry were fighting with the undergrowth, laughing, and shouting for Brian to slow down. But Brian knew where he was going, and nothing would slow him.

At last, the trees thinned and the forest became open to the evening sky. The narrow track Brian had been following had all but disappeared now and he was wading through a sea of undergrowth.

He knew this place.

The pigs and Isabelle, and even Isabelle's tree were all long gone. It wasn't even a proper clearing anymore; trees huddled and brambles grew where Isabelle's soft lawn had once lain. But Brian could feel the memories here, living, and real. He picked his way to where the little house had once been. There was no sign of it now. He scuffed the soil with his shoe where the roots of the hollow tree had once burrowed. Amongst the grass and weeds, his toe bumped something. Without quite knowing why, he bent down and rummaged. His fingers found something cold and hard. Expecting it to be just a stone, he pulled it from the soil. It was a small, glass bottle, filthied by centuries. And inside was a rock which glowed a gentle blue.

Brian felt as if he had reached out through time and touched Isabelle's hand. He was, for the first time, holding something from her world, her time, in his hand.

"For God's sake, Bri," came Terry's voice. "What you doing?" Brian stuffed the bottle into his pocket, wiped his eyes and turned round.

"You alright?" Gary asked. Brian nodded, but couldn't speak. He was grateful for the encroaching darkness which, he hoped, hid his emotion. "Come on," Gary said, "let's head back."

...But Not So Little Boys

And after that, Brian felt lost. He had a vague memory of Dragon saying he could sense fear in him. Brian hadn't understood that back then, but he did now. It wasn't fear of Dragon. It was fear of not belonging in his own world. How could he belong in his own world if his best friend was a dragon in a cave? How could he belong in the real world if his favourite place was another world, and the people he loved were a dragon, a witch and some pigs who didn't even exist anymore?

But he missed them now. Like mad. It was such a long time since Isabelle had gone, and it seemed like forever since he'd first met Dragon. So much had changed since then.

One day, he decided not to go to school. He wasn't sick, but he needed time to think. He told Emily he had a bad stomach, and she said he could stay at home if he promised to help her out with Laura.

But he spent most of the morning in his room, drawing. He hadn't drawn pictures for ages, except diagrams in science. But he really wanted to today. He drew pictures of Isabelle and the pigs, and

Isabelle's house before the fire. He felt like a child again, and he liked that feeling. Just for today. He'd go back to being grown up again tomorrow.

After school, the doorbell went and Brian heard Emily answer the door. He heard Gary's voice, so he quickly hid all his drawings under his bed in case Terry was with him. He wouldn't mind Gary seeing his drawings, but Terry would make fun of them.

His door opened and in came Gary. He threw his coat down on the floor.

"Alright, Bri!" he said.

"Hi," Brian said, trying to sound pleased to see him. The truth was that he'd been about to slip out to go and see Dragon.

Gary sat on the bed next to him. Brian's pens and pencils were still out, and some blank pieces of paper.

"You been drawing?" he said. "You haven't drawn much for ages, have you? I used to love your drawings. Where are they?"

Brian brought the hidden stack of pictures out and let Gary go through them.

"Wow!" Gary said. "That's really good. Look at those pigs!" He stared at the picture. "Look at all the detail," he said. "You've still got the old magic, Bri! It's better than ever!" Then, suddenly remembering something, Gary said cheerily, "Hey, Bri. Did you see the news? See the dolphin? Harry, they've called it. Dunno why. It's got itself stuck in the harbour. It was on TV an' everything!"

"I saw it," Brian said.

"Me and Terry went down there last night," said Gary. "There was a TV van, and cameras filming and things. It was cool." Brian didn't want to think about the dolphin. He remembered the one Emily had told him about, and he felt so sorry for it, but there was nothing he could do. And today he couldn't stop thinking about Dragon. In fact, the dolphin and Dragon were similar: lost, alone, with no friends, somewhere they didn't belong.

"You coming back to school tomorrow, then?" Gary said.

"Might do, depends."

"So," Gary said, "what's really the matter with you? You're not properly ill, I can see that."

"I... I can't tell you."

"Why not, Bri? I'm your mate."

"You'd never believe me. You'd say I was... mad."

"Mad? Why?"

Brian had been thinking about telling Gary his secret. Maybe, if Gary knew Dragon was real, they could go there together, and Dragon wouldn't have to be lonely. It was so hard having to live in two different worlds. Dragon seemed so far away from Brian's everyday life, but if somehow he could bring those two worlds together...

"Will you come with me somewhere?" Brian asked.

"Where?"

"Well... Just come with me. Don't worry, I may be a bit mad, but I'm not a psycho."

Gary smiled. "Come on then."

They grabbed their coats and went down stairs.

"I'm going out, Em," Brian said.

"Oh, Bri, I thought you were going to help me with the washing."

"Later."

Soon they were walking through the rain. Brian led Gary down the hill towards the harbour.

"We might see the dolphin," said Gary, cheerily. Brian nodded.

The sea was grey, and there was white foam on every wave. There were several people in coats and scarves sitting on fishing stools on the harbour wall. They all had huge cameras on tall, three legged stands, and some had green umbrellas set up over them. There were a few children on bikes, or walking with parents. Everyone seemed interested in the water in the harbour.

The car park was half full. There was a grey Landrover with the letters WTV painted on the sides and several huge aerials on top. Its back doors were open and three men were sipping coffee from little cups.

"Everyone wants to see the dolphin," Gary said as they crossed the car park. "Where are we going?"

"Don't worry. It's okay. I'll show you in a minute."

They climbed the hill. It was muddy and cold. They pulled their coats tight round their necks to keep the wind out.

They made their way down, careful of the slippery rocks, and jumped onto the shale.

"What's going on, Bri?"

"It's alright," Brian said. "Follow me." He led the way along the beach.

Just then, they heard the crunch of shale behind them. They turned round, and there was Terry.

"Alright guys?" he called. They didn't reply. "I saw you from the car park. What you doing then?"

"Oh, just came down here for a chat," Gary said.

"A chat? What d'you come here to chat for?" Terry pulled a piece of old wood from the line of seaweed stretched across the beach, and hurled it up in the air. "Look out!" he yelled. They dodged out of the way, and the wood crunched into the shale. "You want to be careful coming down here," Terry said. "The tramp'll get you." He pointed at Brian's cave.

"There's no tramp in there," Brian said.

"Well, you wait 'til you see the drawings then. Everyone reckons some old tramp lives there. He spends his whole life drawing pictures on the walls of his cave."

"You don't know anything about what's in that cave," Brian shouted. "They're *my* drawings!"

Gary and Terry looked at each other.

"What," Gary said. "Did you do those drawings?"

"That's what I said, isn't it?" He was shocked that Gary seemed to know about them too.

"But, we always thought it was a tramp who did them," Gary said.

Brian felt as if the world had just flipped upside down. "Go away. Get away from my cave!"

Terry picked up the piece of wood, and strode towards the cave. "It's not *your* cave, Bri," he said, "We often used to come down here." He looked at the faded drawings around the entrance. "They're quite good, for you." He ducked his head and went inside.

"Get out!" Brian yelled. "Get out!"

"It's alright Bri," Gary said reassuringly, following Terry. "We won't do anything." Brian watched them go into the cave and start climbing about on the rocks, on his pictures. He followed them.

It was pitch dark further in so he pulled the torch out of his pocket and switched it on.

"I can't believe it," Gary said, "I always thought it must have been a tramp."

"Well it's not."

"So," Terry began thoughtfully, "is this where that dragon lived? You know?"

"Shut up."

"Don't look big enough. Dragon's live in big caves don't they?" He laughed, and looked at Gary.

"Leave him alone, Tez," Gary said.

"So, you come here a lot do you?" Terry said. Brian didn't reply. "Ah, Bri, if you want to believe in dragons," Terry went on with a bit of a smirk, "that's fine by me. But I don't, I've got something called 'street cred'."

Brian hated Terry being in the cave, mocking him, mocking Dragon. But there was nothing Brian could do about that. And Terry had been here many times before, so it wasn't such a private, secret place after all. He'd really wanted Gary to meet Dragon, at last, but Terry was here now too. Maybe that wasn't such a bad thing...

"I can show him to you if you like."

"What?" said Terry.

"Come on." Brian climbed up the rock at the back of the cave. It was time they all found out that Dragon was real. Brian got out his torch and slid down into the tunnel. Terry followed.

"What the hell...!" Terry gasped. "A tunnel!"

Brian led him down the dark passage, without stopping to look at the patterns. He could hear Terry tapping the piece of wood against the walls. "Slow down, Bri," he said, "I can hardly see! Shine the torch over here for a sec would you?" But Brian just kept on going.

And then they were in the huge cavern. Terry slipped, and steadied himself.

"Slow down, Bri," he said. "I can't see a thing."

Brian turned and shone the torch on him, and then into the darkness all around. It didn't help much.

But Terry said, "Wow, what a cave!"

"Where's Gary?" Brian said.

"He got scared I think. He's all man you know, apart from the half of him that's woman."

"Hello, Brian," said Dragon. "You are not alone today. Who is that?" Brian looked at Terry. Terry didn't seem to have heard Dragon's voice.

"Hi, Dragon. This is Terry. He's a friend. Sort of." Brian realised they were talking inside their heads. They'd done that so often he hardly even had to think about it anymore.

Or, was it possible Dragon only existed inside his head?

"Is he kind?" Dragon said.

"Well... I've told you about him before, remember?"

"Oh, this is the mean one. I would like to meet him."

Wondering why on Earth he'd never thought to bring someone down here to meet Dragon before, and yet also dreading sharing his secret friend,

Brian lead Terry across the floor of the cavern and shone the torch on the far wall, where the stalagmites barred the entrance to Dragon's alcove. But still he didn't say anything. Terry was right behind him.

"This is amazing, Bri," he said. "Do you always come here?"

Brian peered into the alcove, careful not to shine the torch in Dragon's eyes. Two points of light glinted back at him.

Behind him, Terry, oblivious to Dragon's presence, had launched the piece of wood up into the air. The darkness had swallowed it instantly, of course.

"Look out!" Terry yelled, and Brian saw him dropping to his knees, laughing. A second later, they heard it clatter to the floor somewhere.

"Why did he do that?" Dragon asked.

"I don't know."

"Is he mad?"

"No. He thinks I'm mad though, because I told him about you. He doesn't believe in you."

"Shine the torch over here," said Terry's voice from somewhere behind him. "Brian? Over here." Brian turned and shone the torch over the smooth floor. Terry saw his stick, and ran over to collect it.

"The floor looks man made," Terry said as he came back over to where Brian stood. "What were you lookin' at just then?"

Slowly, Brian shone the torch into the alcove. Terry leaned forward, putting his hands between the stalagmites so that he could get a closer look. Brian could hear Dragon saying, "Hello, Terry," but Terry didn't hear.

All they could see of Dragon was the light in his huge eyes which never blinked.

"What is it?" said Terry, pressing himself against the rock. He peered, squinting into the alcove. "Looks like it's moving..." he murmured. "It looks like... eyes..."

Terry was silent for a few seconds.

"Hello, Terry," Dragon said again. "He can't hear me, Brian."

"I know," Brian said, and then realised that if Terry could have heard Dragon he'd have come down here long ago.

Brian could hear Terry breathing.

He heard him swallow.

Then he heard him say, "Oh my god."

Suddenly Terry made a horrible shrieking noise and began stabbing his stick into the alcove. Brian grabbed him. "No!" he yelled in Terry's ear. "Stop! You'll hurt him!" and they both fell backwards onto the floor. The torch had fallen out of Brian's hand and in its beam Brian saw that Terry's face was full of terror. Terry scrambled to his feet. He stood there breathing in little gasps, then turned and was gone into the blackness.

Brian grabbed the torch and shone it into the alcove. He could hear Terry's running footsteps echoing behind him.

"Are you alright, Dragon?" Brian said. But he could tell Dragon wasn't before he even heard him speak.

"Why did he do that?" Dragon managed, his voice full of pain. From somewhere in the darkness there came a loud smack, and Terry's footsteps stopped suddenly. The idiot had run into the wall. He let out a wordless shout which echoed round the cavern, and the footsteps continued at a more cautious pace.

Brian shone the torch on Dragon's body. He saw the wounds Terry had made. Dark, shiny liquid was running down Dragon's soft, white side.

Suddenly Brian was heaving at the stalagmites. He couldn't move them. He desperately tried to squeeze between them, forcing his shoulders so hard that it hurt. He was too big now. He fell back to the cavern floor.

The Stranger Returns

Terry's footsteps had long since faded so presumably he'd found his way out. Brian didn't care what had happened to him though. All he could think about right now was Dragon's pain.

He was dying.

"I'm sorry, Dragon," Brian said, barely able to control his voice. Even the one in his mind. "I should never have brought him here."

"It's not your fault, Brian. I will never understand people in your world. They do such odd things."

"What if I can get you to a vet? Or a doctor? They'll help you." He stood up and started yanking the stalagmites again.

"They can't help me."

"Someone must be able to help you."

"I was dying anyway, Brian. I know your song says 'Dragons live forever', but we don't. The Magic has kept me alive, sleeping, for so long, but it can't keep me alive forever. The Magic is fading. It's like the power that makes your torch work."

"The batteries?"

"Yes. It doesn't last forever. I need you to get me out... If you can take me to the sea..."

"To the sea?"

"There's something there. A creature. It's in distress, and it's calling for help. Nothing's changed, Brian. I would have asked this of you even if Terry hadn't come here and damaged me. I can't help the creature from here. I must go to it, into the water with it."

"Into the... Can you swim?"

"We moved about in water in the same way as the seagulls move about in the air." Perhaps then, Dragon would be alright if he was in the sea. Again, Brian tried to break the stalagmites apart. He pulled and yanked at them, and thumped them and heaved at them until his hands ached and his fingers stung. But he couldn't break them, no matter how hard he tried. He slid to the floor. It was horrible to think that Dragon had come here to help others, but no-one could help him. Aching inside, Brian stared into the darkness.

Unable to do anything to help, but unable to leave, Brian sat, flicking the torch on and off. His mind reeled with sorrow and confusion. He could sense that Dragon was getting weaker. His voice was fading, and he was making strange noises Brian had never heard him make before. Real noises. Not like his voice which Brian only heard with his mind.

As Brian resigned himself to helplessness, to cold and sorrow, his mind grew numb and began to wander. "How did you get here, Dragon? Into this cave, I mean. How did you escape the crash and find this place?"

"Escape? Find this place?" Dragon laughed, weakly. "I didn't. I have never left the machine I came here in."

Brian was confused by that. Then he realised...

"You mean, we're in it?"

"Yes... though the crash turned it upside down, and pushed it deep into the ground, and nature has tried to take it over ever since."

"Upside down? You mean... I'm sitting on the ceiling in an upside down spaceship?"

"Yes. It was full of water once, and light, and others like me. Hundreds of us, swimming about in here."

Brian had forgotten the awfulness of the current situation as he tried to imagine the spaceship the way Dragon described it, but it didn't last.

"I am sorry, Brian," Dragon said.

"What? Why?" Brian objected.

"Because I failed you."

"No you didn't. Why do you say that?"

"Because you called for help, but my help made you unhappy. I know what has been happening to you."

"That's not true."

"It is true, Brian. You're happy when you're here,

I know that. But in your own world? People in your world don't believe in dragons, do they?"

"Grown-ups don't."

"And you'll be a grown-up yourself one day, Brian. You are changing into one all the time. The Magic woke me, and brought you to me, and us to Isabelle. We helped Isabelle, but I have not helped you. The Magic connected us for a reason, but I failed to understand it. And I have made you unhappy."

"You are my best friend. I'm going to get you out of there," Brian said, giving one last useless tug on the stalagmites. "I'm going to have to go for a little while, but I'll be back soon. I'm going to get you out of there." He stood, and crossed the cavern.

Soon he was running across the car park. It was dark, and the rain stung his face. He ran all the way up the hill, even though his lungs were bursting and his legs were killing him, to his house. The whole time, he could hear Dragon in his head, and he could feel his dying friend's pain.

Upstairs in the bathroom he found what he was looking for. He took the sledge hammer from Dad's tool box and held it under his coat. It was heavy.

Halfway down the stairs, he stopped suddenly, and charged back up to his room. He grabbed the ancient bottle he'd found in the woods, and flew back down stairs, leaping several steps at a time.

He ignored Emily's questions and was soon heading down the hill again.

After a few minutes he was back inside the cave. He crossed the cavern to Dragon's alcove.

He could not believe what he saw. He stood there looking at the fragments of rock, and broken pieces of stalactite which lay on the floor. The alcove was already open.

"What..?"

"An old friend came here," Dragon said. Brian could hear the surprise in his voice too. "He is big now. He pulled the bars down with his hands. Then he went away."

"What friend?"

"The boy I told you about. The boy who was scared of me, who wouldn't ever come close enough for me to help him. Only, he's not a boy anymore. He must have felt my pain. He came to help."

"Where is he?"

"He went out of here. He didn't even look at me. He was strange, but I think I understand him. I could feel his fear. Like yours, only much stronger. He didn't want to come here, but he knew I was hurt. He came to help me."

Brian listened to the darkness, but there were no other sounds. Whoever it was, they seemed to have gone.

"Dragon," Brian said, remembering the bottle in

his pocket. "I've brought this." He was amazed to see the rock glowing brightly, almost dazzling him.

It was a while before Dragon responded. "Brian," he said, "where did you find this?" Brian told him, and added, "I was going to bring it down for you, but Gary was there and I forgot all about it. What *is* it?"

"I remember now. This is pure *life*, Brian. I didn't recognise it before because it has changed beyond recognition. I have never seen it in solid form like this. I remember it as a force, something you can't touch; we had to use our minds to shape it. I can do nothing with it on my own, but when there were many of us, The Magic would guide us and we would create new forms of life from this substance. It has changed, probably because it leaked out into the air. It's no use now, but it is wonderful to see that some of it survives."

Brian stared at the stone, amazed and confused by what Dragon had just told him about it. But at the same time, his heart sank. "I hoped it would help you get better," he said.

Again, Dragon took a long while to respond, and Brian began to wonder if his friend had slipped away. "It... might," Dragon said at last.

"Might it? Can it make you better?"

"We exist to help others. I had never thought of trying to help myself. Perhaps *this* is why The Magic took us to Isabelle," Dragon said after a long, thoughtful silence, and Brian could feel his friend's joy. "The Magic is fading away. It can't keep me alive anymore. But this can."

"Take it," Brian insisted, tipping the rock into his palm. As it touched his skin, he felt a pulse of warm energy surging up his arm: the power Isabelle had mentioned. Dragon extended one of his spider-like limbs and lifted it into the darkness. "Yes, this is why The Magic connected us," Dragon said. "It was to help *me*, as well as you and Isabelle. This will heal me, and give me life outside the cave, when The Magic has died." He seemed to consume it somehow; the glow vanished.

Brian reached into the alcove. He put his arms around Dragon's fleshy body, and felt all the cables and tubes detaching themselves from Dragon. There were little hisses and gurgles as each one came away, releasing him into Brian's arms. He lifted him out. He was surprised that Dragon was so small, and so withered. Yet he was heavier than he'd imagined.

Suddenly the cavern was filled with light. Brian's eyes hurt like mad and he couldn't see.

"What's happening?" he said.

"It is the spaceship, as you called it, just doing what it does. Parts of it still live."

As Brian's eyes adjusted, he saw the light was coming from tiny circles in the walls, circles he had always thought were part of the beautiful patterns and designs. He kept blinking, and screwing his eyes up until he could see properly.

The cavern was as enormous as a cathedral. Its walls were cracked and covered in huge brown streaks and stains. It didn't look like the inside of a spaceship. The walls and floor were straight and flat in some places but twisted and split in others. Rock and tree roots spilled through the splits.

But the lights mostly shone upwards, at the cavern roof—the spaceship's floor—where Brian's torch had never reached.

Hanging from it were some large shapes. They were brown and blotchy and cracked and great stalactites hung from some.

They were sculptures. And they were upside down.

"Animals," he gasped, gazing up at the great mass of creatures: there were huge, four-legged beasts which looked vaguely like elephants, rhinos and wildebeests; there were birds with wide, powerful wings; dinosaurs; fish; dolphins.

"They are the creatures we created. We watched over them," Dragon said. "They changed over time, some of them will have changed into completely new animals. It was... so long ago." Brian remembered he was actually on the ceiling looking up at the floor, and the realisation dizzied him. He looked down at Dragon in his arms. He saw the huge black eyes, like the eyes of a maggot he'd seen in a picture in school. They didn't have pupils, so he could not tell which part of them was looking at him. Maybe they weren't even eyes at all. The light filling the cavern seemed to be dimming now, turning yellow and fading like his torch beam. In the dying light, he saw Dragon's white flesh, wrinkled like Brian's toes and fingers after a long hot bath. He looked at the stick-like feelers which waved about at the air. He saw Dragon's mouth open and close slowly; it wasn't like a human's mouth. He knew the voice he loved hearing did not come from this mouth which was made of three hairy, toothless flaps, each one covered in tiny spines. One of the flaps moved up and down, and the other two moved from side to side like double doors. And the hole behind them was dark and fleshy, and there were little worm-shaped things around the edge of it wiggling about in there.

The sight of Dragon made Brian feel sick. He was Brian's friend, his *best* friend, yet suddenly, part of him wanted to drop him to the floor.

There were thick, spiny legs, like spiders' legs all along Dragon's belly, and they waved about and snagged against Brian's coat. There were puckered, grey holes along Dragon's back, presumably where wires and cables had been attached. Dragon was like an insect lava that had been pulled out of its chrysalis before it was ready. Brian was thankful that the light had almost died away now.

He carried the heavy creature up the tunnel. As they left the cavern, the lights sputtered out, and it seemed to Brian that it wasn't just the lights which had died. The whole place seemed to give out one last dying breath, and he knew that Dragon could not have stayed here. The Magic, which had sustained Dragon for thousands, probably millions of years, in his strange form of sleep, had finally run out. But it had saved him too, by connecting him with Brian and Isabelle.

Carrying Dragon, Brian struggled over the rocks in the dark cave. He slipped down the last few on his bottom.

"I don't want you to go," Brian managed.

"I have to, Brian."

It was dark and raining, and Brian didn't even notice the cold.

"I can feel the cry for help, it's very close now," Dragon said.

Brian's eyes blurred. He carried Dragon across the beach and up over the slippery rocks, his arms starting to shake from the weight.

There was someone there in front of him. It was a tall figure standing alone in the car park.

Brian could see who it was straight away. But he

couldn't believe his eyes.

He blinked hard to squeeze the stinging tears away. He looked again.

He stared, speechless.

As he approached, his father didn't say anything either, but he put his big arms under Dragon's belly, and helped Brian to carry him. He looked at Brian for a moment, and neither of them knew what to say.

Together, they headed down to the water's edge. The cars had mostly gone, as had the big trailer that the news people had brought down. The gravel of the car park crunched under foot.

"The cry is near now," said Dragon.

Keeping to the darkness against the rocky spur which divided the car park from the shale beach, Brian and his Dad carried Dragon along seaweed-strewn rocks and boulders. They stopped when they reached the end, and looked down at the dark waves.

"The cry is coming from there," Dragon said. "In the sea."

"Please," Brian said. "Please, come back won't you," and his voice sounded nearly as weak and shaky as Dragon's.

"Tell him…" Dad said, "tell him to keep away from fishing nets and… and propellers and things." Brian nodded, and quickly passed the warning on.

In the dark water a small fin broke the surface some way off, then disappeared.

Brian and his Dad picked their way down the rocks until their feet were in the water and the cold waves splashed against their ankles.

"Goodbye, Brian," Dragon said. "You have saved me. Thank you."

"Goodbye..." was all Brian was able to say.

Carefully, they lowered him into the sea. They watched him float beside them for a little while. The dolphin surfaced again, quite close this time. Brian gazed at it for a moment. When he looked back at the water by his feet, Dragon was gone.

He felt his father's arm round his shoulder. They stood there for a very long time. They didn't speak. Brian could feel Dragon near at first, but slowly he felt him fade away.

Dragon and Isabelle's Gift

Losing Dragon hurt Brian as much as losing Emily or Laura or Mark or Dad would. It was like losing his Mum all over again. But at least he knew Dragon was alive, somewhere out there with the dolphins.

And, strangely, Brian felt as if he had something new. He felt as if his life had changed. In fact, things had first started to change when Laura was born. Without even knowing it, Laura seemed to have made everybody different. Home became a happier place when she arrived.

But home had still been far from perfect.

Until now.

Now, Brian's dad shared his secret. He knew Dragon was real. It didn't matter anymore what other people thought.

That awful night, it was Gary who had come to the rescue again. When Terry had burst from the cave, bleeding, crying and seemingly half mad, Gary knew he had to do something. He followed Terry for a while, trying to get some sense out of him. He had blood all down his face from where he'd run into the wall, and he wouldn't, or couldn't speak to Gary. So Gary left him and hurried back to the cave, too scared to go in, but worried too about Brian. At last, he decided he had to tell someone. He was about to head back up the hill to get Emily or Mark when he realised Brian's dad might be in the pub. He might not be the most reliable of parents, but at that moment he was certainly the closest. And, they realised when they talked about it later, Brian must have gone home in search of the mallet just when Gary went into the pub.

A few days after they said goodbye to Dragon, the news reported there had been no more sightings of the dolphin and scientists were hoping it had found its way back out to sea. Emily was delighted, of course, and was even talking about having a party to celebrate.

Brian's dad called him a hero. He said it was him who had done it: saved Dragon and saved the dolphin. For the first time ever, Brian felt his dad was actually proud of him. And interested in him.

Dad even said Brian had saved *him* too.

One evening, they even walked together in the woods by the playing field, and Brian told his dad all about Dragon, and Isabelle, and all their adventures. Brian's sadness at losing Dragon swelled in him, but now it was mixed with a glowing feeling, a sparkling excitement for those wonderful times. These were the very woods where Isabelle had lived, unrecognisable now of course, but full of the same magical beauty he had come to love. He could almost hear the pigs lumbering through the bracken and the brambles; he could almost smell the smoke from Isabelle's fire and hear her laughing.

And was it his imagination, or could he feel Dragon at his side again?

His dad seemed transfixed by his tales. And he believed every word. Of course he did, because he had been the boy on the beach all those years ago. He'd heard Dragon's call, but had been too old, too grown up to accept that the creature in the cave could possibly be real. But now he knew.

"I should have let Dragon help me all those years ago," Dad said as they ambled aimlessly through the trees. "But I couldn't, Son. That voice in my head scared the hell out of me, I can tell you. Thought I was losing my mind."

"All Dragon wanted to do was help," Brian said. "It's like he was an angel. Not a dragon."

"Funny-looking angel." They both smiled. "Mind you, funny-looking dragon! I could've used a friend back then though, when my dad was... when he was... treating my mum so horribly." It shocked Brian to hear his dad talking about that, even though he knew from Emily something of what his grandfather had been like. "He was horrible to her, Bri. I was too old not to notice, but too young to know what to do about it. I felt useless. My dad made me... made me so... angry!" Brian had never heard his dad talking like this before. "Been angry ever since; all my life, until I met your mum. We made a family, a wonderful family, and... I got scared. Scared of being useless and scared of being like him. And then your mother died and I fell apart. I know I've let you down so badly, Son."

"No, Dad," Brian said, even though he knew his dad was right.

"I'm ashamed of myself. I want you to know that. I used to think the drink makes the shame and the troubles and the uselessness go away, but it doesn't. It just makes it all feel worse."

"You're not useless, Dad. Isabelle said that even good people do bad things sometimes. But good people feel sorry afterwards and try to change."

"I've hurt you, though. You, Emily; I should have been a proper parent, like your mum was." He wiped a raindrop from his eye. "I'm gonna do it, son. I'll kick the drink and be a proper dad. For you."

"Do it for Laura, Dad."

"For all of you. Will you help me? I'll need your help."

"How?"

"Just..." Brian heard his dad's voice crack. He took a deep breath, then tried again. "Just tell me you forgive me."

Around them, the trees breathed. Brian felt sure his friends were here, ghosts in his world as he had once been in theirs.

"Of course I forgive you, Dad."

And that, Brian suddenly realised, was Dragon and Isabelle's gift to them both.

Epilogue

"I don't know what you did to Terry," said Gary as Brian arrived at school the next day. "He had blood all down his front. He wouldn't say anything to me about it, he just ran off. I hope you didn't mind that I went after him, he just looked like he needed me."

"It's okay," Brian smiled, "I think he probably did need you."

"He said he bashed his head or something, but he wouldn't tell me how. Did you thump him?"

"No, he ran into the wall."

"Did he? Woh! Something got him scared then. What was in there?"

Brian had known that sooner or later Gary would ask him that, and he'd spent ages thinking about what he should say. But he'd never quite decided. So, when he opened his mouth to speak he didn't really know what was going to come out.

"My friend the dragon," he said, grinning. Gary laughed, and said, "That's your story and you're sticking to it, I suppose?"

"Definitely!"

They put their bags down on a dry bit of the playground and started to kick the ball around.

Some more boys arrived and joined in. Then Terry arrived.

"Wow!" gasped Roger when he saw the plaster across Terry's nose. "What happened?"

"I fell over." He glanced at Brian, then at the other boys.

During lessons that day, Terry seemed to be keeping right away from Brian and Gary, but at dinnertime he came up to Brian in the cloakroom.

"I suppose you think you're clever," he hissed. "What was it? A cat or something?"

There was a part of Brian that hated Terry.

But there was another part to him now too. He knew Isabelle had done something terrible when she was younger. He remembered those men coming to get her, to kill her. And he knew that if he hurt Terry because of what he had done, he would be like those men.

Besides, Terry had had the shock of his life. That was going to stay with him for a very long time. Longer than his broken nose. Maybe forever.

"That was Dragon," Brian said assertively.

Terry shook his head. "All your stories got me on edge," Terry said. His voice sounded as if he was holding his nose. "But I'm not a mental case like you." He took his coat and went outside. Brian stood there, feeling cross with himself for not having said anything clever to Terry, to put him in his place.

There must have been a thousand things he could have said, but he'd not been able to think of them. Just like usual.

And now he was missing Dragon more than ever. But there was also a new emotion in him today. Something that blotted out any irritation Terry caused. It was a bubbling spark of excitement and in his mind he saw his dad smiling at him.

The door opened, and Gary came through.

"Alright Bri?"

He nodded.

"Listen," he said. "Don't take any notice of Terry. He's full of rubbish. I mean, he's a mate and everything, but, don't let him wind you up." He smiled. Dragon would have liked Gary.

"Thanks," Brian smiled back.

"Come on. We'll meet the boys down on the field." Gary picked up the ball. "Race you!"

More great books by Antony Wootten

A Tiger Too Many

Jill is deeply fond of an elderly tiger in London Zoo. But when war breaks out, she makes a shocking discovery. For reasons she can barely begin to understand, the tiger, along with many other dangerous animals in the zoo, is about to be killed. She vows to prevent that from happening, but finds herself virtually powerless in an adults' world. That day, she begins a war of her own, a war to save a tiger.

"Real edge-of-the-seat-stuff." TheBookbag.co.uk

There Was An Old Fellow From Skye

A collection of Antony Wootten's hilarious limericks for all the family to enjoy. Featuring everything from King Arthur and his knights to inter-stellar space-travel, There Was An Old Fellow From Skye is packed with tiny tales which will tickle the ribs of children and adults alike.

"This is a little pot of gold with lots of clever rhymes guaranteed to make you laugh."
LoveReading4Kids.co.uk

You might also like these books by Antony's father, Paul Wootten:

The Yendak **by Paul Wootten**
Christer has shared most of his young life with his cousin Sophie. But when Sophie becomes desperately ill, his aunt hopes that the sound of Christer's voice might help to bring her round. He visits, as promised, and embarks on a quest for the mind of his cousin, lost somewhere in another dimension. Following clues in her diary he plunges into a strange world of oppressed people, ruled by the Yendak, a cruel and violent race. If they find him, he will never get back home.

Whispers on the Wasteland **by Paul Wootten**
Tim has spent the last few years of his life travelling from place to place, following his father's job. He rarely stays long enough to make any friends, and now he's come to Wattleford where a patch of wasteland is marked for development. A natural playground for the children, it has, over the centuries, sheltered humans and wildlife among its trees and shrubs. Tim finds himself strangely in tune with the peoples of the past, but the town council has plans to develop the wasteland. Modern machines bring destruction and change, and Tim and his father are all that stand in their way.

You can find out more at
www.antonywootten.co.uk.